INTO THE JAWS OF DEATH

Nate parted the weeds quietly, his nerves on the raw edge, his eyes darting right and left. Seven yards into the strip he noticed a break in the vegetation a few more yards in front of him. Puzzled, he warily stepped forward until he could see that the break was actually a drop-off, the top of an earthen bank that blocked from his view whatever lay below.

Exercising extreme caution, Nate moved closer to the rim of the bank. He heard a guttural cough, then the distinct whine of an infant. The baby was down there! Eager to save the child, Nate dashed forward and took in the scene twelve feet below.

The mountain lion stood in the middle of a secluded gully. At its huge feet rested the cradleboard. The lion was eyeing the baby hungrily and might tear into it at any moment.

Nate took a hasty bead on the cat's head, hoping to end the menace with one shot. He began to steady his rifle when he felt his left foot slip out from under him. Startled, he realized he was going over the bank....

The *Wilderness* Series Published
by *Leisure Books:*

8

WILDERNESS

Death Hunt

David Thompson

LEISURE BOOKS NEW YORK CITY

Dedicated to —
Judy,
Joshua,
and Shane.
And to Scott Kendall,
a great guy.

A LEISURE BOOK®

January 1992

Published by

Dorchester Publishing Co., Inc.
276 Fifth Avenue
New York, NY 10001

Chapter One

"Do you reckon we have everything we'll need?" asked the muscular young man in buckskins.

The lovely Indian woman to whom the question had been addressed looked at their packhorse, her features barely concealing her keen amusement. "We have enough supplies to last a year, husband," she said and grinned. "Any more and that horse will keel over." She glanced at him. "That is the right expression, yes? Keel over?"

"It's the right one, Winona," the man responded a bit testily.

Ever sensitive to his moods, Winona moved closer and affectionately reached up to caress his cheek. "I am sorry if I hurt your feelings, Nate."

Nineteen-year-old Nathaniel King softened under the loving gaze of her dark eyes. He shrugged his broad shoulders and gestured at the assortment of parfleches, saddlebags, and other supplies piled high on the pack animal. "I'm taking so much because of the condition you're in. Who knows what we'll need along the way? It will take seven or eight days to reach the village, maybe longer."

Winona glanced down at the highly prominent bulge in her beaded buckskin dress, then pressed both palms to her swollen belly. "There is no need to worry. Our son will not be ready to enter this world for fifteen or twenty sleeps yet."

Nate put his hands on his hips and regarded her critically, extreme anxiety mirrored in his penetrating green eyes. In addition to his buckskins, he also wore moccasins and a brown leather belt. Wedged under the belt, one on either side of the large buckle, were two flintlock pistols, and suspended in a sheath on his left hip was a big butcher knife. Angled across his chest were a powder horn and a bullet pouch. "You can't say for certain when the baby will come, and I'd rather not take any chances. What if you go into childbirth before we find the village? We'll wind up stranded in the middle of nowhere until you're back on your feet. That could take days."

"What nonsense," Winona said lightheartedly, as she smoothed the flowing raven tresses that fell to her hips. "I will be able to ride the day after our son is born. There will be little delay."

A sigh of exasperation hissed from between Nate's lips. He simply couldn't understand his wife's cavalier attitude; she seemed to view giving birth in the same manner as she did eating and sleeping, as a bodily function that would pretty much take care of itself and wasn't any cause for concern. "If I had any sense, I would have taken you to St. Louis to have the baby," he said.

Blinking in surprise, Winona stared eastward, out over the verdant valley in which their sturdy cabin was situated, and watched a flight of ducks come in for a landing on the aquamarine surface of the tranquil lake a stone's throw away. The mere thought of traveling to one of the strange cities Nate had told her about sent a chill of apprehension rippling down her spine. Much of what he had described was incomprehensible—vast tracts of land covered in haphazard fashion with countless stone and wood lodges separated by narrow passages called streets, all swarming with the ceaseless activities of more people than there were blades of grass. To her, to a Shoshone woman accustomed to the orderly, quiet life of an Indian village, the sprawling cities of the whites seemed to be the embodiment of insanity, at odds with the way of Nature and the Great Medicine. "Why would you have taken me there?" she wondered.

"Because a woman should have the best medical help available when she gives birth," Nate said, turning to his black stallion. He began checking the cinch. "This is 1829, after all. It's not like we live in the Dark Ages. A modern doctor would make sure everything came out just fine."

Winona grinned. "Everything will come out just fine without a doctor. Women have been having babies since the dawn of time and human beings have not died out yet."

Nate glanced at her. "I wish you would take this seriously. You don't know how worried I am."

"Yes, I do," Winona assured him. "And I know you worry because you love me." She felt the baby kick and beamed. "But you worry too much, husband."

Finishing with the cinch, Nate walked into the cabin. He knew better than to debate the issue. They had been through it again and again with the same result. She simply refused to become in the least bit anxious about the birth. Fine and dandy, he reflected. At least he'd been able to talk her into visiting her relatives at a Shoshone village far to the north where there would be other women who could lend a hand just in case something did go wrong. Although, when he thought about it, she had agreed a bit too readily, as if she had wanted to visit her kin all along and was merely using his anxiety as an excuse to go. How typical, he thought. Women were the most devious creatures on God's green earth. They always got their way, no matter what their men might prefer. Why was that? Why did men always fall for feminine ploys? It certainly couldn't be because the men weren't as smart.

He retrieved his Hawken from the large table on which he had placed it an hour earlier after loading it. The feel of the heavy rifle snug against his palm heartened him slightly. The trip would take eight or nine days, perhaps more. They were bound to run into contrary critters and maybe a few hostiles. The Hawken would come in handy; next to the horses, it was the most indispensable item they were taking.

Nate gazed around the interior, making sure they had packed everything he wanted to lug along, then went outside and closed the door behind him. The morning sun hung above the snow-crowned peaks rimming the eastern horizon, and there was a cool nip to the early April air.

Winona had already mounted the mare she would ride and held the lead to the pack animal.

"I'll take that," Nate said, walking toward her.

"I am not helpless," Winona said, giving the lead a tug as she brought her mare around to face due north.

"But you're pregnant," Nate objected.

"You are an observant man, husband," Winona said and snickered.

Annoyed, Nate mounted his stallion and moved out, passing her. "I don't see why you must be so stubborn. I'm only trying to help." He headed for a gap in the mountains, thinking about the route they must take, remembering where water existed and planning his stops accordingly. A person could go without food, if need be, for weeks, but anyone who went without water for more than three or four days stood a good chance of perishing. So, like the Indians, he would camp each night near water and start each morning refreshed and revitalized.

"Do all white men act like you do when their women are heavy with child?" Winona inquired.

"Most, I guess," Nate said, wondering what she was leading up to. "Why?"

"I would expect it."

Nate glanced over his shoulder. "Oh?"

"From the stories you have told me and those I heard when I was younger, I know white men treat their women very strangely. You treat them like dolls."

"Dolls?"

"Yes," Winona said in her precise English. She had spent months mastering the language, and now she took great pride in pronouncing every word distinctly. "Among my people it is a custom for mothers and other relatives to make dolls for the little girls to play with. I had three dolls when I was a child, all from my mother. She even made clothes for them to wear and built a small lodge for them to live in."

"I don't see the connection," Nate said.

"I treated my dolls very carefully because I was afraid they would break," Winona elaborated. "Every day I dressed them in their fine clothes and had them do all the things real women would do, but I never let them get dirty or was rough with them."

"I still don't see the point."

"Don't you?" Winona responded. "White men treat their women just like I treated my dolls. You keep them in great lodges and dress them in fancy clothes. You let them rear the children and take care of the lodge, but you never let them do any of the work the men do. You act as if they will break if they do anything a man does."

"That's not necessarily true," Nate said. "And you're a fine one to criticize the way white men live. When was the last time you went on a buffalo hunt?"

"I never have and you know it."

"And why not?" Nate asked and promptly answered his own question. "Because Indian men don't let their women hunt big game or go on a raid or do most of the things men do." He paused. "I guess when you get right down to it, Indian men aren't much different from white men."

"In some respects they are much alike," Winona agreed wistfully.

"Does that upset you?"

"I always wanted to go buffalo hunting or be part of a war party," Winona said. "But I did not complain when my father told me I could not. My father loved me very much, and it was my duty as his daughter to obey his wishes."

Nate looked at her and detected a tinge of melancholy in her expression. "Tell you what," he said impulsively. "After the baby is born, the two of us will go after buffalo."

"You would do that for me?"

"Of course."

Winona brightened, then burst into laughter.

"What is so funny?" Nate asked.

"Who will watch our baby while we are off chasing buffalo?"

"I don't know. I hadn't thought of that," Nate admitted. "Maybe we'll have to wait until the baby is old enough to tag along."

They fell silent, Nate pleased with himself for having made such a considerate offer. But the more he thought about it, the more convinced he became that he'd made a rash mistake. What if Winona was injured, or worse? Hunting buffalo was a tricky, extremely dangerous task. Many warriors died each year doing so. Next to being slain in battle, more Indian men died from hunting the shaggy brutes than from any other cause. Since Winona had no experience at it, she would be at even greater risk. Perhaps, Nate concluded, he should come up with a reason for her to not do it. Something logical, something devious. And if that failed, maybe she'd agree to go after elk or deer instead.

He scanned the surrounding landscape, alert for movement or noise. They were crossing a boulder-strewn field between tracts of dense woodland. Chipmunks chattered at them or darted off at their approach. Far overhead, to the west, sailed a large red hawk, its wings virtually motionless as it glided on the air currents seeking prey. In the brush to the east a black-tailed buck appeared and watched them for a minute before bounding away in great leaps.

Nate inhaled and smiled. This was the life! He could hardly believe that only a year earlier he'd left New York City to join his Uncle Zeke in St. Louis and, through a series of unexpected events, had found himself joining the slim ranks of those hardy trappers and adventurous mountain men who chose to dwell in the Rocky Mountains. He had, as the saying went, "gone native," and he didn't regret the decision one bit.

Only out here, in the unspoiled wilderness where men could roam as they pleased and live as they wanted, was there true freedom. His Uncle Zeke had promised him a share in the greatest treasure any man could ever find, and Nate had to admit his uncle had been right. Freedom was more precious than all the money in the world, than all the gold and gems in existence.

Thinking of Zeke brought to mind his father and

mother, and Nate felt a twinge of guilt at having left them so abruptly with no more than a note of farewell. Did they miss him? Did they wonder if he was alive or dead? He speculated on the wisdom of contacting them, perhaps sending a letter back east with the next person he met who was heading that way. At least they would know he was all right.

They would also probably despise him for what he had done. After all, his father had refused to allow Zeke's name to be mentioned in their house after Zeke ventured beyond the frontier and never came back. That had been a decade before Nate left New York. To think that his father had nurtured such keen resentment for over ten years made him see his father in a whole new light. Zeke had been his father's brother. How could a man hate his own brother?

Nate shook his head to dispel the bothersome thoughts and skirted a boulder the size of a pony. It was too late to have regrets, he figured. He'd made the decision to leave New York on his own, and he would have to live with the consequences for the rest of his life.

Twisting, Nate gazed fondly at Winona, who gave him a smile. If he had not headed west, he would never have met his wife, and he considered her the best thing that had ever happened to him. She brought genuine happiness into his life, helped him to smile when he was depressed and to confront hardships squarely. For her, he would do anything. And he didn't give a damn whether his folks would approve of the marriage or not.

There came a time, he reflected, when every man and woman must strike off on their own, must leave the nest just like little birds eventually left theirs to take up the responsibilities of adults. Well, he'd simply gone a lot farther from his nest than most did, and the rewards justified the deed.

Nate saw Winona passing a cluster of small rocks on her left. He spied a flash of movement near a rock tilted upward at an angle and figured her horse had spooked a chipmunk. But then he saw a sinuous shape glide into the open and coil for a strike. The next moment, as he realized with horror what it was, he heard the distinct rattling of its tail.

Chapter Two

Rattlesnake!

The word peeled like the loud clanging of a fire bell in Nate's mind, and he reined the stallion around to bring his Hawken into play.

Startled by the rattler's buzzing, Winona's mare started to rear up, its nostrils flaring, whinnying in alarm. Winona yanked on the reins, trying to turn her mount to the right away from the deadly reptile.

A terrifying mental image of Winona being thrown filled Nate with fear. If she went down, they might well lose the baby! He whipped the Hawken to his shoulder and took a hasty bead on the rattler's head. Its forked red tongue was flicking out and in, its tail vibrating vigorously. He cocked the hammer, held the barrel as steady as he could, and squeezed off the shot.

At the booming report, a cloud of smoke burst from the rifle as the lead streaked true to the mark, the ball hitting the rattler between the eyes and coring the brain. The snake flipped onto its side and thrashed wildly, blood and brains oozing from the thumb-sized hole in its shattered cranium.

Nate hardly gave the rattler a second glance. His wife was still striving mightily to bring the mare under control while holding onto the lead to the packhorse, which was trying to jerk free. He goaded the stallion to her side and leaned over to grip the mare's bridle. "Whoa, there. Calm down. Calm down," he said in a soothing tone.

The mare—the same horse he had ridden all the way from New York to the Rockies and then presented to Winona because the animal was normally supremely gentle and obedient—reacted to his voice by standing still and bobbing its head, its eyes wide, still afraid but compliant.

Winona turned her attention to the pack animal, hauling on the lead with both hands and speaking to the horse in Shoshone. "The snake is dead, silly one. Be still."

It took all of ten seconds, but the packhorse stopped trying to bolt and stood as quietly as the mare.

Nate looked down at the motionless snake, then at his wife. "Are you all right?" he asked in her native tongue. He had spent as many hours trying to master Shoshone as she had mastering English, but he was not half as proficient at her language as she was at his.

"I am fine," Winona said and placed a hand on her belly.

"Are you sure? What about the baby?"

"Our son kicked to let me know we disturbed his nap," Winona replied, grinning.

Nate let go of the mare, moved closer, and placed a hand on her shoulder to draw her face near to his. He gave her a tender look, glad she was unharmed, thinking of how she always took everything in stride, how she seldom became agitated or anxious. He wished he had a smidgen of her self-possession. She was gazing at him with a puzzled expression. Nate chuckled, then planted a passionate kiss full on her soft lips before she knew what he was going to do.

When he pulled back, Winona stared at him in surprise. "Why did you do that?"

"My heart overflowed with love," Nate answered in Shoshone and climbed down. Having learned many months ago that a man in the wilderness must always keep his rifle loaded because trouble had a habit of popping up when least expected, he quickly reloaded the Hawken. First he placed the butt on the ground, then he poured the proper amount of black powder from his powder horn into the palm of his hand, knowing by sight exactly how much to use. He carefully poured the powder down the barrel, then took a ball and a patch from his ammunition pouch. Wrapping the ball in the patch, he wedged both into the end of the barrel with his thumb. Next he pulled the ramrod free, then pushed the ball all the way down.

"Do you want to save the snake for a meal later?" Winona asked. "I can wrap it in a blanket and skin it when we stop."

Nate glanced at the dead reptile. Although rattlesnake meat was highly extolled by many of the trappers, the mere thought of eating one made him slightly queasy. If he had been without food for a spell, he'd tear into a rattler with relish. But given a choice, he'd rather eat rabbit or venison or *anything* that didn't slither to get around. "I'll bag us something else," he promised her and slid the ramrod into its housing under the rifle barrel. Swinging into the saddle, he grasped the reins and headed northward again.

Soon they were at the gap, riding between towering cliffs on either side, the path steeped in deep shadow, the wind whistling shrilly past them.

Nate craned his neck, staring at huge boulders perched precariously on the rims of both cliffs, dreading what might occur should one suddenly come crashing down. He recalled a tale he'd heard about a trapper who was leading a pack string down a winding mountain trail when a ten-ton boulder swept down out of nowhere and slammed the man and his horse right over the edge. The trapper's friend, who witnessed the freak accident, went down to see if there was anything he could do and reportedly found the trapper crushed to a pulp, unrecognizable. A shudder rippled through Nate at the memory.

He breathed deeply in relief when they were in the valley beyond, delighted at the warm sunshine and the chirping of birds in the forest to their left. A narrow stream, fed by a spring high in the mountains, meandered across a grassy meadow before them, and he stuck to the bank, watching to see if there were any fish in the water.

"May I ask you a question, husband?" Winona spoke up.

Nate recognized a formal tone in her voice, a tone she used only when she felt she might be prying into his personal feelings and was reluctant to broach whatever subject she had in mind. "Ask away," he said.

"Do you think of Adeline often?"

"I should have known," Nate muttered and chided himself for ever having mentioned Adeline to Winona.

The daughter of one of the wealthiest men in New York City, Adeline Van Buren had been the epitome of beauty and charm and could have taken her pick of any man she wanted for her husband. To Nate's unending astonishment, she had chosen him. They'd met at one of those boring social functions the upper crust so delighted in putting on, and an immediate attraction had led to their avowed intent to marry. In retrospect, Nate knew his love for her had been more in the order of awed devotion; he'd practically worshipped her. He'd placed her on a pedestal a mile high and had constantly reminded himself that he was the luckiest mortal alive simply because he was so unworthy of her affection. All she had to do was snap her fingers and he was at her beck and call.

How strange, he reflected. Back then he'd believed he was truly in love. Now, with the benefit of hindsight, he saw how foolish and immature he'd truly been. Comparing his love for Adeline to his love for Winona was like comparing night and day. He loved Winona as she was and related to her as an equal instead of as a supplicant before a goddess.

When he'd departed New York to go join his Uncle Zeke, he'd written Adeline a letter in which he'd promised to return one day with a great fortune. He'd wanted to be able to support her in the same lavish fashion her father always had; it was the main reason he'd left everything behind to venture west.

Had she found someone else by now? Nate wondered. Most likely. Suitors would have lined up for blocks once word of her eligibility spread. No doubt her father hated Nate. But that couldn't be helped and didn't bother him all that much because he had never been fond of her father anyway.

Should he write her another letter? No, he decided. She must resent the way he had gone off and left her; sending a letter would only spark bitter emotions. It was best for him to forget about her and get on with his life, which was hard to do with Winona bringing Adeline up at least once a week.

"Do you think of her?" Winona repeated when he failed to answer right away.

"No."

"Then why did you take so long to say so?"

Nate glanced back. "When will you get it through your pretty head that you are the only woman I care for? If I still loved Adeline, I wouldn't have married you, now would I?"

"I have heard about white men who take Indian women as wives for a winter or two, then leave them to go back to families the Indian women never knew they had."

"Do you think I could ever do such a thing?"

Winona locked her eyes on his as if trying to peer into the depths of his soul. "No," she admitted softly. "You are a good man."

"And you are the one I want to start a family with," Nate said. "You and our children will be all the family I need. I'll be your husband for as long as you want me."

Her mouth curled upward. "Then you will be my husband forever."

"Now that we've settled the matter for the twentieth time, do you suppose we can drop it for good?"

"I am sorry if I upset you."

"You didn't."

They pressed onward in awkward silence. By midday both had forgotten the discussion, and they chatted and laughed while taking a break beside a spring situated at the base of a bald mountain.

Sunset found them many miles farther along, in dense woodland. Nate scoured the terrain ahead, seeking a small lake he'd stumbled on previously. He was certain the lake must be close by, and a quarter of a mile later his hunch was confirmed when they emerged from the trees and discovered the serene body of water before them.

"I'll tend to the horses, start a fire, and go find us something to eat," Nate proposed as he rode to the water's edge and dismounted.

"And what should I do while you are taking care of everything else?" Winona asked.

"Rest," Nate said. "You must be tired after being in the saddle all day."

Winona sighed. "When will you learn? I am all right.

You go hunt while I take care of the horses and the fire."

Knowing a protest would cause an argument, Nate resigned himself to the inevitable and headed toward the forest 40 yards to the south. Twilight shrouded the landscape, bathing everything in a shade of gray. He glanced back to see his wife watering their animals, then peered at the trees and detected a flicker of movement out of the corner of his left eye. Halting, he looked and spotted a large jackrabbit bounding for the shelter of the vegetation. It was moving slowly, covering only five feet at a hop. On every fourth or fifth leap it would jump several feet into the air, giving itself a better view of him and the surrounding ground.

Nate pressed the Hawken to his right shoulder, recalling information imparted by Shakespeare McNair, the gray-haired mountain man who was his best friend and mentor. "If you spook a rabbit," Shakespeare had said, "stand stock-still and get ready. They usually stop after going a short ways and look back to see if they're being chased."

He hoped his friend was right. If he could bag the jackrabbit, it would save a lot of time and effort. Taking careful aim, he tracked the rabbit's course. After only four more bounds it abruptly stopped and stared at him.

Now!

Nate squeezed off the shot and saw the jackrabbit flip into the air, then slam into the ground hard and commence flopping around. He ran toward it, drawing his butcher knife, preferring to save his twin flintlocks for an emergency.

The ball had struck the hapless rabbit in the neck, and it now lay still on its side, blood gushing out, its eyes flared in panic.

Swiftly, Nate stooped over and plunged the blade

into the yielding body, putting the animal out of its misery with one stab by piercing the heart. The jackrabbit quivered for a bit, uttered a low squeal, and died. Watching it expire, Nate thought of the rabbits he'd raised as a child back in New York and felt a twinge of guilt. "Sorry, bunny," he said softly. "But I have two mouths to feed besides my own."

He yanked the knife free, wiped the blade clean on the rabbit's fur, and slid the weapon into its sheath. Grasping the rabbit by the rear legs, he stood and carried his trophy toward the lake. He guessed its weight to be nine or ten pounds, which would more than suffice to feed them.

Winona had turned at the crack of the shot and was waiting for him, smiling proudly. "That did not take long," she said as he drew closer.

"I was lucky," Nate replied. He dropped the rabbit on the grass and began reloading.

"I will skin it as soon as I have the fire started," Winona said and headed for the trees.

"Where do you think you're going?"

"To get firewood."

Nate gazed at the gloomy woods and changed his mind about objecting. "Let me take care of fetching branches while you hobble the horses and get the rabbit ready," he suggested. "To his surprise, she halted, glanced at the forest, and came back.

"All right. But please be careful. I have a feeling."

"What kind of feeling?" Nate asked.

"It is difficult to describe. A feeling all is not well."

Nate surveyed the countryside but saw no sign of danger. "I'll take care," he promised, hoping his wife's intuition was wrong. After loading the rifle, he hastened off, eager to gather the wood they would need before night fell. A cool breeze from the northwest stirred his hair. He was almost to the forest when the air was rent by an eerie, drawn-out howl arising on the far side of the lake. Nate stopped in mid-stride. Seconds later another howl sounded, then a third and a fourth. An icy hand seemed to gouge into Nate's stomach and twist his innards as he swung around in alarm.

A wolf pack was abroad!

Chapter Three

Nate had a decision to make. Should he keep going or go back to Winona? He didn't like the notion of leaving her alone with wolves in the vicinity. Although wolves rarely attacked humans, he knew from bitter experience that a pack would do so if the wolves were hungry enough. A few months ago he'd nearly lost his life in such an incident. He weighed the need for a fire against his guess that the wolves were still a quarter of a mile away and kept going. A roaring fire would keep most animals at bay. Once he had their campfire blazing, the pack would leave them alone.

Finding enough broken limbs was easy. Nature's tantrums and old age had scattered scores on the forest floor. Nate swiftly collected enough to fill both arms and hastened back to the lake. As he neared the horses, the wolves howled once more. Winona was busy at work on the jackrabbit. "Did you hear that?" he asked anxiously.

"How could I not?"

"They might be coming in this direction," Nate said, selecting a spot to start the fire. He deposited the branches and straightened. From the continued howling, he deduced the pack was moving slowly along the west shore. His stallion whinnied and tried to stamp the ground with a front hoof but the hobble prevented its leg from lifting very high.

Nate stepped to the big horse and opened his possibles bag, which hung from the saddle horn. He rummaged inside and found his tinderbox, then set about starting a fire as he continued listening for the approaching pack. They were yipping as well as howling, and he marveled at the noise they were making.

It took the better part of a minute to ignite the kindling, and then another minute to fan the tiny flames with his breath until they rose over six inches high. He fed small pieces of dry wood to the fire and soon had the campfire roaring in all its comforting glory.

The wolves promptly fell silent.

Nate stood, the tinderbox in his left hand, the Hawken in his right, and looked at his wife. "If those wolves should attack, stay behind me."

"I do not think they will," Winona said, removing the last fold of skin from the butchered rabbit. "They are talking to the moon is all."

The moon? Nate gazed eastward and was surprised to behold a radiant full moon perched above the horizon. Shakespeare had once divulged that wolves and coyotes voiced their plaintive cries much more frequently on moonlit nights than they did on nights when the moon was absent. Why, no one knew.

He replaced the tinderbox in the possibles bag and scanned the southwest corner of the lake, wondering if the wolves would come very close or be intimidated by the fire. He saw several inky shapes flitting over the ground and swept the rifle to his shoulder. A second later the shapes halted and seemed to be regarding the campsite intently. A huge wolf advanced much closer, the firelight dancing in its eyes, making them glow a reddish hue.

Winona had also seen the pack. "Throw him the rabbit skin," she said.

"What?" Nate responded, surprised by the suggestion.

"That big one is the leader of the pack. As a token of good will, take him the skin and a little meat."

"And leave you here alone? Not on your life," Nate said.

"Trust me. My people have been dealing with wolves for more winters than anyone can count. If you do not want to do it, I will."

"No," Nate said, moving to her side. He stared at the motionless pack, counting six lupine forms, and envisioned the consequences should Winona go out there and be wrong about the wolves' intentions. "I'll handle it."

Winona picked up the skin and a handful of meat. "Here. Go out a ways and put this on the ground."

Nate took the rabbit parts in his left hand, feeling the meat squish against his palm and blood seep between his fingers. Dismayed but striving hard not to show it, he advanced toward the predators with his left arm extended. What if they detected the smell of fresh blood and came for him? he wondered. There was no way he could down them all before they reached him and ripped him to ribbons.

The wolves promptly backed away, warily keeping their distance, not taking their eyes off him. Last to back off was the leader, and he only went a dozen yards before stopping.

Nate walked to the spot where he believed the big wolf had stood and squatted to put down his offering.

Loath to touch the rifle with his gore-covered hand, he wiped his left palm on his pants before rising and backpedaling to the fire. He scarcely breathed while waiting to see what the pack would do.

The leader of the pack cautiously moved forward. When it came to the rabbit parts, the wolf sniffed loudly, then swallowed the morsels in three gulps.

"What if he wants more?" Nate asked.

"That is the whole idea," Winona said.

"Mind explaining it to me?"

Winona spoke softly. "By giving him the rabbit skin, we have whetted his appetite. Now he is hungry for more meat and he will lead his pack off to find it."

"Or attack us."

"Why must you always expect the worst?"

"Experience," Nate said. "If anything can go wrong, it usually will."

Suddenly the big wolf wheeled and loped off into the enveloping darkness, the other wolves right behind him. They disappeared without another sound.

Nate expelled a breath, then chuckled. "Your little trick worked." He paused. "You don't happen to have one that works on grizzly bears, do you?"

"No."

"Too bad. The way I keep running into them, I could use an ace up my sleeve."

The next several hours were spent enjoyably. Nate unsaddled their horses and removed the packs from their pack animal while Winona roasted tasty portions of jackrabbit by imbedding slender forked branches on either side of the fire and impaling the meat on a straight stick supported by the forks. By the time Nate finished with the horses, the tantalizing aroma of their impending meal filled the air and made his stomach growl with hunger.

They savored the food, slaking their thirst with cold water from the lake. A multitude of twinkling stars covered the heavens, and they saw several shooting stars while they ate.

Afterwards, Nate spread blankets on the ground and stacked limbs near the fire so he would have a ready source of fuel to use during the night whenever the fire started to die out. They reclined side-by-side and he pulled another blanket over the two of them. "This is nice," he said.

Winona nodded and kissed him on the cheek, and they cuddled together for a while, whispering as they discussed plans for their future and their hopes for the child soon to be born. More fatigued by the arduous traveling than she was willing to admit, Winona fell asleep first, nestled in Nate's arms. He beamed happily, pulled the blanket higher, and drifted asleep thinking that he must be the luckiest man on the planet.

Dawn etched the horizon with a rosy hue when Nate awoke and sat up. As always when in the wilderness, he made a quick survey of their camp to ensure all was in order. The horses had not wandered very far, due to the hobbles, and were munching on the dew-covered grass. A fish jumped in the lake, splashing down loudly and causing concentric circles to ripple outward from the impact point. Off to the east were several deer eyeing the camp. Apparently they had been on their way to the lake for their morning drink, but were now reluctant to approach.

Nate stretched, inhaling the crisp, invigorating mountain air. He slid out from under the blanket, being careful not to disturb Winona, and attended to his toilet. Then he collected the horses, saddled the stallion and the mare, and got the pack animal ready to go. He heard a rustling noise as he completed the job and turned to find Winona sitting up and gazing around in annoyance. "Good morning, honey."

"I slept too long," Winona said. "The sun is already

rising. You should have woken me up."

"You needed the extra rest," Nate said, going over and squatting by her side.

"A person should never sleep past sunrise. It makes them lazy," Winona stated, running a hand through her hair.

"My, aren't you the grump this morning?" Nate quipped and kissed her.

"Grump? What is that? I do not remember hearing that word before."

"A grump is someone who is always in a bad mood. They always look at the bad side of things."

Winona seemed shocked. "Am I truly a grump?"

"Not in the least," Nate assured her, grinning. "I was only making a joke."

"You should work more on your sense of humor," Winona admonished him.

"Yes, dear," Nate said dutifully and kissed her again. He gave her a hand as she began to climb out from under the blanket, gazing in awe at her huge belly. "What do you want for breakfast?"

"Nothing."

"Not a thing? We have jerky and bread in our supplies. Why not start the day with a full meal?"

"Because my stomach is not feeling well," Winona said, straightening with a frown.

Nate didn't like the sound of that. Her bouts of morning sickness had ended months ago. This new feeling might have been brought on by all the riding they had done, and he berated himself for being a fool, for lugging her scores of miles across the Rockies in her present condition. She should be back in the cabin, snug in their bed, and he told her as much.

"Nonsense," Winona replied. "A woman who lies around all the time becomes weak and no good as a wife. It is too late to turn back, anyway. I am looking forward to seeing my aunt and her family."

The reminder prompted Nate to nod. In his concern he'd almost forgotten the reason for the trip; he certainly didn't want his wife giving birth by herself. "All right. I'll finish packing everything and we'll be ready to go when you are."

In ten minutes they were heading northward again, journeying through virgin wilderness overflowing with game. Nate used the time to improve his Shoshone so he would make a favorable impression on Winona's tribe. She enjoyed giving the lessons, her patience inexhaustible, correcting him repeatedly and laughing at some of his grammatical blunders.

At midday they stopped briefly, then went on.

During the afternoon, as they were crossing a ridge that barred their path, Nate reined up in surprise at the sight of smoke curling above the trees half a mile to the west. "Look," he said.

Winona did and said, "A campfire."

"Might be Indians," Nate said.

"It could be white men. Trappers, maybe."

"I'm not about to risk finding out," Nate said, goading the stallion down the opposite side. "If it's Utes, they'll kill us, take my hair, and mutilate you. We keep going."

"Yes, husband."

Nate picked up the pace and was glad when they had put a few more miles behind them. His safest bet was to avoid all other parties they saw until they reached their destination. If they should be seen by hostiles, they would not be able to outrun enemy warriors with Winona in the family way. "Lie low and live longer," Shakespeare had once advised Nate concerning travel in hostile country, and he intended to follow the advice to the letter.

Evening found them by a small spring at the base of a rocky escarpment, and Nate halted for the night. Despite his usual protests, Winona insisted on taking care of their animals. He went into the forest to bag their supper and was fortunate in spying several large, plump mountain grouse in a thicket. By bracing the barrel of the Hawken against a tree trunk and taking careful aim, he shot the biggest of the bunch and proudly took the kill back to their camp.

Unlike the previous night, there were no nocturnal visitors. They ate their meal in peace and were soon tucked under their blankets, admiring the magnificent celestial display. Slumber claimed them and they slept until dawn in each other's arms.

And so it went.

For the next four days they made steady progress. Game was abundant and they ate their fill each night. Twice they spotted grizzly bears, but fortunately the fierce beasts were at a distance and didn't charge them. They saw no sign of other humans, Indians or whites.

On the afternoon of the seventh day, as they were skirting a mountain that towered over ten thousand feet above them, Winona unexpectedly reined up. "We must stop for a while," she announced.

Nate stopped, then turned the stallion. He noticed her features were drawn, her eye betraying great fatigue. "We'll rest for as long as you want," he said, sliding down.

"I am sorry," Winona said wearily. "The trip has been harder on me than I figured it would be. I am slowing us down."

"Nonsense," Nate said, leaning the Hawken against a nearby boulder. He reached up and lifted her to the ground. "You've held up fine. And by tomorrow we should be at the lake where your people are supposed to be camped at this time of year. You can lie down for days if you want."

Winona sagged against him, her cheek on his chest.

"I am sorry to be such a burden."

"Don't be silly," Nate said and stroked her hair. "You're the best wife a man could ever want."

Smiling, Winona looked up at him. "There are times when you are the most wonderful man I have ever known." She kissed his chin. "And then there are times when you are the most hardheaded man who ever lived."

"Which am I now?" Nate asked, grinning.

Winona opened her mouth to reply, her gaze straying past him, and suddenly she involuntarily stiffened and gasped.

Nate let go of her and spun, spying the source of her alarm immediately. Thirty yards off, sitting astride a fine brown stallion and watching them intently, was a lone warrior.

Chapter Four

Nate scooped up the rifle and pressed the stock to his right shoulder, about to take a bead on the man when he realized the warrior wasn't making any threatening moves. The man simply sat there, studying them.

"He is a Dakota, but I do not know which tribe," Winona said. "The French call his people the *Nadowessioux*."

Nate had heard the term before. Some of the trappers had taken to referring to the Dakota people by an abbreviated version of the French word: the Sioux. "I thought the Sioux live far to the east of here, on the plains," Nate said, noting the warrior appeared to be in his thirties and wore buckskins leggings and moccasins, but no shirt. The man carried a shield bearing the red emblem of a bird of prey on his left forearm and a lance in his right hand. A bow and a quiver full of arrows were slung over his back.

"They do," Winona confirmed. "They seldom come into the mountains."

Nate glanced right and left, seeking other warriors, certain the man was a member of a war party in the region on a raid. But he spied no one else. Perhaps, he reasoned, the others were lying in ambush.

The Sioux abruptly started toward them.

Not about to let the warrior get close enough to hurl the lance, but unwilling to fire unless provoked, Nate sighted his rifle squarely on the man's muscular chest. Instantly, the warrior reined up. Nate lowered the Hawken a few inches, debating whether to try sign language to communicate. To do so, he would have to lower the Hawken all the way, delaying his reaction time should the Sioux charge.

The warrior glanced at both of them, then placed his lance across his legs and lifted his hands. "I will not harm you," he signed.

"Should I trust him?" Nate asked, relying on Winona's superior knowledge of Indian ways to guide him.

"Not yet," Winona said.

Nate saw the warrior was awaiting a reply. He shifted and extended the Hawken toward his wife. "Here. Keep me covered while I talk to him."

"If he tries to lift his lance, he is dead," Winona promised, grasping the rifle and taking deliberate aim. Under Nate's tutelage she had learned to be a fair shot and could down small game at over 50 yards consistently.

Loosening the flintlocks under his belt, Nate advanced ten feet and addressed the Sioux in the universal language of the Indian tribes inhabiting western North America. From Canada to Mexico, from the Mississippi River to the Pacific Ocean, practically every tribe used sign language, with minor variations in different areas. And since their spoken tongues were so diverse, sign had long since become the accepted means of communication when people from far-flung tribes met. "What do you want?" Nate asked.

"I am Red Hawk of the Oglala Dakotas. I would talk with you," the warrior answered.

Was it a ruse? Nate wondered. There was only one way to find out. He beckoned for the man to approach, saying, "You may approach, but be warned our guns are loaded and we will shoot at the first sign of hostility."

"I come in peace," Red Hawk said and rode forward.

Nate held his hands near his flintlocks. If it was a trap, he'd take as many of the Sioux with him as he could. Fleeing was out of the question with Winona in the condition she was in. A sustained flight over the rough terrain might kill her and the baby.

The Dakota appeared at ease and made no threatening gestures as he narrowed the gap.

Nate noticed symbols painted in red on the warrior's horse. Six horizontal lines had been etched on its neck, and on its flank was the likeness of a human hand. "What are those marks?" he asked Winona.

"The lines mean he has counted coup six times," she said. "The hand means at least one of his enemies was killed in hand combat, either with a knife, a tomahawk, or a war club."

"Oh?" Nate said, edging his fingers a tad closer to his pistols. He still saw no sign of any other Dakotas, which mystified him. It was inconceivable that the warrior was alone.

Red Hawk halted ten feet out and extended his hands to demonstrate they were empty. "How are you known?" he inquired.

"I am Grizzly Killer," Nate responded, feeling grateful to the Cheyenne warrior who had initially bestowed the name on him. At times like this it had a nice ring to it. "This is my wife, Winona."

"A Shoshone," Red Hawk signed, nodding politely at

her. "My people have fought the Shoshones a few times. They are brave fighters."

Nate decided to be blunt. "Where is the rest of your war party?" he inquired, gazing around.

"I am alone," Red Hawk said, frowning.

Skeptical of the claim, Nate said, "It is very dangerous for a lone Dakota in this territory. The Utes, the Blackfeet, the Crows, and perhaps even the Shoshones would kill you on sight."

"I know," Red Hawk signed. "But it is just as dangerous for me east of the mountains where the Arapahos, the Cheyennes, the Pawnees, and my own people would do the same."

"Your own people?" Nate repeated, adding the hand signal for a question. "I do not understand."

"I am an outcast."

The revelation surprised Nate. He'd heard that certain tribes would cast out members if various customs or taboos were violated, but the offense had to be extreme to justify such a severe punishment. He speculated on whether it would be polite to request the details.

"If you are willing, I would like to ride with you for a while," Red Hawk said.

"We travel by ourselves," Nate quickly replied, unwilling to let the warrior go along and thereby possibly put Winona's life in jeopardy.

"Please," Red Hawk said. "I have given you my word that I will do you no harm." He paused. "I have not talked with anyone in many sleeps. It would be nice to have the company of other people again, if only for a little while."

Nate hesitated. He believed the man was being sincere, but his innate wariness compelled him to balk at the notion. A tactful way of getting the Dakota to move on occurred to him, and he signed, "We are very near a large Shoshone village. Should the Shoshone warriors find us, they might slay you."

"I no longer care," Red Hawk answered. "At least I will not be alone when I die."

About to make a frank refusal, Nate felt Winona press flush with his back and heard her whisper in his ear.

"It is all right, husband. I think you can trust this man."

"Very well," Nate signed. "You may accompany us. But you must ride at my side the whole time."

"I understand," Red Hawk said, "and agree."

Nate took the Hawken from Winona. "Do you still want to rest for a spell?"

"No. Let us move on. I am eager to reach the village."

Casting repeated glances at the Dakota, Nate assisted his wife in mounting the mare, then swung onto the stallion. They moved out, the warrior falling in beside Nate's horse. Up close, he observed that Red Hawk appeared to be much younger than he had estimated.

"I thank you for this privilege," the Sioux signed, his face conveying genuine gratitude.

Nate got the impression his newfound acquaintance was literally starved for human companionship. "Do you happen to speak any of the Shoshone tongue or the language of the white men?"

"No."

"No matter. We will get by with sign language."

"You use it very well," Red Hawk noted, "better than any white man I have ever met. Most of the traders and trappers I have known learn just enough to get by."

They moved out into a wide valley, riding northward across a verdant meadow. A raven flew past them, uttering its raucous cry at their intrusion into its domain.

"These mountains stir the spirit," Red Hawk said.

"My people prefer the plains, where most of the buffalo roam. But now I think these mountains would be a fine place to live."

"There are plenty of remote valleys, far from any tribe, where you could set up a lodge and live happily. Most of the time it is quite pleasant in the high country, but The Long Night Moon, the Snow Moon, and the Hunger Moon can be bitterly cold and it is sometimes hard to find game then," Nate signed, referring to the harshest months of the year—December, January, and February.

"I doubt I will ever have a home again," Red Hawk said. "My fate is to wander the land until I die."

The warrior wore a melancholy expression as his hands moved, and Nate experienced a twinge of pity although he hardly knew the man. He tried to imagine what the life of an outcast was like—always on the go, considered an enemy by his own tribe and every other tribes besides, unable to go near any village without risking the loss of his life, banished to a lonely existence with the sole prospect for the future being eventual death. He tried to cheer the man up by pointing at the coup stripes and signing, "You must be a brave warrior to have counted so many coup."

"Four were earned in one battle when the Blackfeet raided our village and tried to steal our horses," Red Hawk responded, gesturing crisply in a matter-of-fact fashion. "I killed one of them with my knife after he had stabbed me." He touched an inch-long scar on his lower right side.

"The Blackfeet do not die easily," Nate signed by way of a compliment. "Your people must have been very proud of you."

A shadow clouded Red Hawk's features. "Yes, they were. My wife was the proudest one of all."

"You have a family?"

"I had a wife once, and we often talked of having

children. Now I will never have either."

What did that mean? Nate mused, but he didn't pry. He scanned the meadow, where the grass grew as high as their horses' bellies, and spied a butterfly flitting to the southwest.

"I have thought of going north into the land you call Canada," Red Hawk said. "Have you ever been there?"

"Not yet," Nate signed. "One of these days I will get around to it. For now, I am kept busy providing for us and trapping. If all goes well, by the Blood Moon I will have many pelts I can trade or sell for much money."

Red Hawk pursed his lips. "I have noticed white men are very fond of money. Why is that?"

"A person cannot survive for long in the white world without it," Nate explained. "Whites use money to buy food and clothes and horses and weapons."

"I do not see the sense in such a strange way of living. Why should whites pay money for food when they can hunt for it or grow their own?"

"Some whites do grow food, and they provide enough for those who do not grow it to live," Nate signed. "Those who do not grow food pay money to those who do for the food they need."

"And why do whites pay money for clothes when making clothes is so easy? All they have to do is go out and kill a buffalo or a deer, work the hide until it is soft and can be sewn together, and they will have clothes that last many years," Red Hawk said.

"Many whites, mainly those who live in the big towns and cities, do not know how to hunt. They have never shot an animal in their life."

Red Hawk looked at Nate in amazement. "How can such a thing be?"

"They buy the clothing they need," Nate said.

"And their weapons too, you said?"

"Yes," Nate affirmed. "Although in many of the cities back in the East men have no need for them."

"They go around unarmed?"

"Yes."

"I have never heard of such a thing," Red Hawk signed, shaking his head in disbelief. "Your people are lucky to still be alive."

Nate smiled, idly gazing out over the high grass. The stallion suddenly raised its head and sniffed loudly, then snorted.

"Now I understand why your people love money so much," Red Hawk remarked. "They would die without it."

Again the stallion snorted and looked to the right and the left, as if seeking something. Nate surveyed the meadow but saw nothing to explain his mount's peculiar behavior. The big horse was acting as if a predator was in the area. Perhaps, he reasoned, the wind had carried the scent of a prowling panther or some such animal.

Winona's mare also snorted and balked, and she had to goad it forward with her knees.

"Something is wrong," Red Hawk signed. His own war-horse began behaving skittishly.

What could it be? Nate wondered. Abruptly, the grass ended at the rim of a huge depression and he had to rein up sharply to avoid going over the edge. He looked down into the bottom of the eight-foot-deep hole and felt the hairs at the nape of his neck tingle. For there, lying on her side on the bottom, sound asleep, was an enormous female grizzly. He knew it was a female because lying beside her, flush with her massive form, were two young cubs likewise asleep. All three had probably gorged themselves recently and were sleeping off the stupor brought on by their filled bellies.

Nate heard a gasp and glanced to his right to find Winona staring at the beasts in horror. He'd heard of trappers who had stumbled on sleeping grizzlies and lived to tell about it by quietly hastening elsewhere before the fierce bears could awaken. Consequently, he motioned for Winona and Red Hawk to move away from the rim, but no sooner had he done so than Red Hawk's horse whinnied loudly and the female grizzly opened her eyes.

Chapter Five

The instant the she-bear laid eyes on the riders above her, she scrambled to her feet and vented a horrid roar that exposed her large, razor-edged teeth.

"Run!" Nate shouted in English, forgetting in the intense excitement of the perilous moment that Red Hawk wouldn't be able to understand the words. He saw Winona cut to the right to go around the depression and did the same, staying behind her to cover her should the grizzly pursue them.

Red Hawk was going around on the other side.

Startled into wakefulness by their mother's roar, the two cubs were on their feet and bawling in terror. The mother rumbled deep in her chest and surged out of the hole, her powerful muscles rippling under her golden-brown coat of fur. She paused on the rim and glanced both ways, apparently undecided about which way she should go.

Nate hoped the she-bear would let them depart in

peace even though his past dealings with grizzlies had
convinced him they would go after anything that
moved. Females with cubs were especially dangerous;
they would even attack other grizzlies who presumed
to get too close to their offspring. This one proved to be
typical of the breed.

The mother bear uttered another mighty roar and
charged after Nate and Winona.

Could they outrun the beast? Nate wondered. The
mare and the pack animal were going all out and his
stallion was right on their heels. If he wanted, he could
make the stallion go even faster and easily escape, but
he would never desert Winona. He glanced back,
watching the she-bear run, marveling that such a huge
creature could move so rapidly.

Out of the corner of Nate's eye he saw Red Hawk
turn his war-horse and gallop toward the depression
housing the cubs. The Sioux gave the grizzly a wide
berth. Amazed, Nate saw the she-bear slow, her attention diverted to the warrior for a few seconds. What in
the world was the man trying to do? he mused. But his
thoughts were interrupted when the bear came swiftly
toward him and his wife again.

Red Hawk was almost to the hole when he stopped
and started whooping at the top of his lungs, waving
his lance overhead.

The she-bear twisted her head, saw the warrior in
close proximity to her offspring, and suddenly forgot
all about chasing Nate and Winona. Spinning, the
grizzly raced to save her cubs.

"Get out of there!" Nate shouted in Shoshone, afraid
the warrior was about to sacrifice himself so they
could escape safely. He saw the she-bear draw closer
and closer to the hole, and just when he thought Red
Hawk would surely die, when the bear was within four
or five bounds of the Sioux's mount, Red Hawk angled

the horse to the west and took off like a bolt of lightning.

The she-bear reached the depression and stopped at the rim, glaring about her in primal fury. She took a few steps after Red Hawk, then halted. Growling hideously, she lumbered ponderously to the hole and vanished from view.

Once she was gone, Red Hawk swung northward again.

"Hold up," Nate shouted to Winona and brought the stallion to a halt beside her, within a few dozen yards of a tract of woodland. "Are you all right?" he asked.

Winona took a breath and put a hand on her belly. "I feel a little sick, but otherwise I am fine."

"We should find a spot for you to rest a spell."

"No. Please," Winona said. "We are close to the village. I just know it. If we stop, we might not get there until tomorrow and I would rather spend tonight in a warm lodge than sleep on the cold ground."

Nate could rarely refuse her anything. Her pleading tone, combined with the silent appeal mirrored in her eyes, made him go against his better judgment and say, "If that's what you want, we'll keep going. But if you feel any pain, any discomfort at all, you're to let me know and we'll take a break. Fair enough?"

"Yes," Winona said, smiling gratefully.

Pounding hooves brought Nate around to face the Dakota as Red Hawk rejoined them. "That was a very brave thing you did," he signed.

"My horse can fly like the wind. I was in no real danger," Red Hawk responded, giving his mount a pat on the neck.

"I know better," Nate said, "and I thank you for risking your life so that we might get away. I hope one day I can repay the favor."

"There is no need," Red Hawk signed.

They resumed their journey, the incident with the grizzly largely forgotten, just another happenstance in the daily lives of those accustomed to living in the harsh wilderness and coping with the occasionally savage wildlife. After traveling for over an hour, a high hill appeared in their path.

"I know that hill," Winona said to Nate. "It is near Clear Lake where my people will be camped."

Nate picked up the pace, eager to get his wife out of the saddle and resting on soft robes. When they reached the hill he spied a game trail winding up the slope and took it, riding all the way to the top where a magnificent vista of the surrounding countryside unfolded before his appreciative gaze. He beamed happily upon spying a large body of water a mile and a half off to the northwest. Even at such a distance the sprawling collection of lodges rimming its shores was visible although they appeared to be little more than tiny peaked cones, with thin columns of smoke spiraling skyward above them.

"The village," Winona said, smiling.

Red Hawk glanced at Nate. "It is time I rode on by myself. Thank you for your company," he signed. "Should we ever meet again, I will remember you as a friend."

"Wait," Nate impulsively signed. He didn't like the idea of the Dakota wandering aimlessly over the Rockies, with nowhere to call home, the war-horse his sole companion.

About to turn his horse, Red Hawk paused.

"Come with us to the Shoshone village," Nate said. "I will ask Winona's aunt to put you up with us."

"You are kind," Red Hawk said, "but her people and my people have never been on friendly terms. As you mentioned before, they might kill me on sight. It is best if I leave you now."

Nate looked at Winona, hoping she would speak up

and try to persuade the Dakota to stay, but she said nothing. In exasperation he watched Red Hawk ride off to the southwest. "This isn't right," he said. "Why didn't you say something?"

"You know why. If he went with us, nothing I could say or do would stop my people from doing him harm."

Frowning, Nate started down the opposite side of the hill. Sometimes, he reasoned, life could be extremely unfair. Red Hawk had impressed him as being a fine person, yet the warrior had been banished to a lonely life of quiet desperation. What could the Dakota have done to deserve such a fate?

At the base of the hill they entered a maze of pine trees, threading among the conifers until they came to a wide field. A doe, feeding near the tree line to the east, bounded into the underbrush.

Winona rode on her husband's right side. She studied his features, as ever sensitive to his moods, and said, "You are upset."

"Only because I wanted to help Red Hawk," Nate responded wistfully. "Surely there must be a tribe somewhere that would take him in? He doesn't deserve to be an outcast the rest of his life."

"How do we know what he deserves?" Winona said. "We have no idea why he was made an outcast. Perhaps he committed a horrible deed."

"Maybe," Nate said. But somehow he doubted such was the case. In any event, the issue hardly mattered now that they had parted company with the warrior. He focused on the village ahead, feeling a twinge of nervousness at the prospect of being among the Shoshones again. Not that they would mistreat him. They were always courteous and kind. There just was an unnerving aspect to being the sole white person among hundreds of Indians. He couldn't help but see himself as an outsider. "What's the name of your aunt again?" he inquired to take his mind off entering the village.

"Morning Dove," Winona said. "Her husband is named Spotted Bull. They have a son, Touch The Clouds, who has a wife and two children of his own. And they have a daughter called Willow Woman who once had a husband named Brown Leaf. She lives with them now."

"What happened to her husband?" Nate asked. "Did they go their separate ways?" He knew that many tribes indulged in lax marriage practices. Among the Shoshones a man could simply tell his wife to leave. Among the Cheyennes, a woman could divorce her husband merely by moving back in with her parents.

"No," Winona said sadly. "Brown Leaf was killed on a buffalo hunt." She paused, then said meaningfully, "On a surround."

"A what?" Nate asked.

"A surround is the greatest of all buffalo hunts," Winona elaborated. "The warriors close in on a buffalo herd from opposite directions, driving the animals into a large circle. Then the warriors charge from all sides and slay as many as they can. The buffalo fight fiercely, using their horns to rip open men and horses. More warriors are killed in surrounds than in any other kind of hunt."

Nate could see why. He'd hunted a few buffalo and had learned to respect their formidable size and nature. A full-grown bull stood six feet tall at the shoulders, weighed about two thousand pounds, and possessed wicked curved horns capable of tearing into a horse and rider with the same ease a knife sliced into butter. "You'll never catch me going on a surround," he said.

"I am most happy to hear that," Winona said. "I would dislike losing you so early in our marriage."

Nate looked at her and saw she was grinning.

Suddenly, from off to the left, arose loud whoops. He faced in that direction and discovered seven riders galloping toward them, Shoshone warriors who were shouting and waving their weapons overhead. He reined up and gripped the Hawken in both hands.

"Look who is in the lead," Winona said.

Studying the foremost Shoshone, Nate smiled when he recognized the tall, lanky form of Drags The Rope, a young warrior he had met months ago. He relaxed and waved, glad to see his friend again.

All seven of the riders were young warriors, all dressed in buckskin shirts or no shirts at all and buckskin leggings. All were well armed with bows, war clubs or tomahawks, and lances.

"Greetings, Drags The Rope," Nate called out in their language as they approached.

The tall warrior blinked in surprise as he brought his horse to a stop. "Grizzly Killer!" he exclaimed in English. "You have learned our tongue much well."

"Thank you," Nate said, recalling that a mountaineer known as Trapper Pete had taught Drags The Rope a little English over six years earlier and now the warrior liked to converse in it every chance he got. "I've had an exceptional teacher," he said and indicated Winona.

One of the other young warriors, a stocky youth who wore a perpetual smile, inquired in Shoshone, "Have you killed any grizzlies since last you were with us, Grizzly Killer?"

"Just two," Nate answered.

The warriors exchanged amazed expressions and Drags The Rope laughed.

"*Only* two?" the tall man said in his own language. "Some of us go our whole lives without killing one. If you keep going at this rate, there will be none left in these mountains in a few years."

The others erupted in hearty mirth.

Nate smiled with them. One of the Indian traits he most admired was their keen sense of humor. Even in adverse circumstances they invariably found humor. Indians, he had learned, were rarely as grimly somber as many whites often were, and their refreshing, naturally joyful attitude appealed to him. He often wished he could develop a similar outlook on life.

Drags The Rope glanced at Winona. "Soon you will be a father," he said.

"Very soon," Nate agreed, keeping his voice level so he wouldn't betray his anxiety over the impending birth. "How about you? Have you taken a wife yet?"

"No," Drags The Rope said. "Soon, I hope. I have been walking under the robe with Singing Bird, and I believe she will agree to be my wife before the next moon."

"I'm happy for you," Nate said, recollecting his own courtship with Winona. A common romantic practice among several tribes was that of permitting courting couples to stand under a buffalo robe and whisper sweet words to each other, or the young lovers might be allowed to go for short moonlit strolls while wrapped in the same robe and, if they were lucky, they would be able to sneak a few kisses. Heavy fondling, however, was strictly frowned upon, viewed as an insult to the girl that could get the prospective suitor in a lot of trouble if she complained. Fortunately, few girls did.

"If you are here when she says yes, you will be welcome to my lodge for the celebration," Drags The Rope said.

"You honor me."

Drags The Rope gestured to the southwest. "We are on our way to hunt deer or elk. Would you like to come along?"

"Another time, perhaps," Nate said. "We must get

settled in. It's been a long ride and Winona is very tired."

"Later then, my friend," Drags The Rope said and led the small band off at a gallop. They screeched and shouted in wild abandon, hot-blooded youths eager for adventure.

Nate watched them depart, remembering how it was to be reckless and without a care in the world. Then he looked at Winona, at the bulge in her dress, and swallowed hard. Even though he was not yet 20, those days were over for him forever. Now he had responsibilities, and he must face up to them as best he knew how. Squaring his shoulders, he headed toward the village.

Chapter Six

The Shoshone encampment presented a fascinating spectacle. Three hundred and sixty lodges were spread out to the east and south of Clear Lake. Varying in size depending on the wealth of the owners, all the lodges were made of meticulously dressed buffalo skins. Children scurried among them, the boys conducting foot races, shooting small bows, or playing games while the girls played with dolls or assisted their mothers. Women were everywhere, engaged in the many tasks required of them, from cooking to preparing rawhide to drying meat and repairing torn lodge skins. The men, for the most part, were either talking in groups, tending to their horses, or else gambling with buffalo-bone dice.

The Shoshone clan to which Winona belonged had adopted many of the ways of the Plains tribes, the Cheyennes, the Arapahoes, and the Dakotas. There were other Shoshones who still lived much as had their ancestors, subsisting primarily on fish, roots, berries, and seeds. This second branch of the Shoshone people lived farther west and rarely ventured after buffalo, which had become the focus for the eastern Shoshones' very existence. They depended on the great brutes for the food they ate, the clothes they wore, and for the lodges that kept them warm at night.

Curious glances were cast in Nate's direction as he approached the village with Winona at his side. Such a large number of lodges meant that numerous smaller bands, usually composed of those with family ties to one another, had gotten together for a mass reunion, an event that transpired only two or three times a year. Because it was difficult to find enough game to keep so many mouths fed, most of the time Indians preferred to travel in smaller bands.

"Any idea where we'll find your aunt's lodge?" Nate asked.

"None at all," Winona answered. "We will have to ask around until we find someone who knows."

An elderly warrior with white hair came toward them, walking with a slight limp. "Welcome, white man," he said to Nate in Shoshone. His gaze strayed to Winona. "Have you come to join our gathering?"

"Yes," Nate replied, halting. "Do you happen to know where we might find the lodge belonging to Spotted Bull?"

The warrior seemed surprised at Nate's fluency. "Yes, I do. I have known him for years," he said, pointing to the north. "It is near the lake within a stone's throw of where we stand."

"Thank you," Nate said and headed off. What luck! He noticed a few boys were trailing behind, studying him and whispering among themselves. White men elicited as much curiousity among Indians as Indians did among whites.

"At last," Winona said. "I am excited about seeing my aunt again. She is a sweet woman."

Nate didn't bother mentioning the profound relief he felt at having Winona among her kin again. Now she would have help when the baby came and he could breathe a lot easier. He surveyed the lodges nearest the lake. They formed an uneven line, each separated by 20 or 25 yards from its neighbor. The third one bore the painted likeness of a great bull buffalo with light-colored spots on its back. "Let me guess. That must be the one we want," he said.

"You are learning," Winona said with a smile.

As they neared the entrance an attractive woman in her early to mid-twenties emerged from the lodge carrying an empty parfleche in her left hand. She looked up, saw Winona, and uttered a squeal of delight. "Cousin! Is it really you?"

"Willow Woman," Winona declared happily and rode up to her relative before dismounting.

Nate reined up. He leaned on the saddle horn and idly watched the women exchange heartfelt greetings. The commotion brought two other people out of the lodge, a woman in her fifties and a slim warrior sporting streaks of gray in his hair, who then greeted Winona with as much enthusiasm as Willow Woman had. The words were flying so thick and fast that Nate had a hard time keeping abreast of the discussion. Finally Winona turned to him.

"I almost forgot. This is my husband, Grizzly Killer," she said sheepishly. Then she indicated the man and the older woman. "This is Spotted Bull and Morning Dove."

"I am honored to meet both of you," Nate said, sliding down. He realized a half-dozen Shoshones, on their way southward, had stopped to observe the pleasantries and he began to feel as if he was being examined under a magnifying glass. To his surprise, Spotted Bull stepped forward and squeezed his shoulders.

"I am the one who is honored," the warrior said. "I have heard much about you." He gazed past Nate. "Since you do not have a lodge, I insist that you stay with us for as long as you like."

"We are grateful," Nate said. "My wife needs to rest after our long trip."

Spotted Bull glanced at the three women, who were chatting away, and grinned. "She will be occupied for a while. If I know women, and after fifty-six winters I know them as well as a man can, she will rest when she is ready. Come, I will help you unpack your horses and show you where to tie them."

Although Nate would rather have insisted that Winona lie down, he couldn't bring himself to make an issue of it when she was so happy at being reunited with her relatives. With Spotted Bull's assistance he removed their belongings from the pack animal, unsaddled both mounts, and took everything into the lodge. Nate grabbed the three hobbles he had made from rope out of a pack, then Spotted Bull helped him lead his horses around to the rear of the lodge where nine others were grazing contentedly.

"You may leave your horses with mine," Spotted Bull said. "There is plenty of grass and water here."

"How long have you been at this spot?" Nate asked as he hobbled his stallion.

"Twenty sleeps," Spotted Bull said and looked out over the village. "It is a good gathering this year. I have seen friends I have not talked to in many winters."

Nate went about hobbling the mare and the packhorse, and when he straightened he saw a bemused expression on the warrior's face. "Did I do something funny?"

"Do your horses wander off often?" Spotted Bull asked and pointed at the hobble on the mare.

"I don't give them the chance."

Spotted Bull gestured at his own animals, none of

which were hobbled or ground-hitched. "I train them to always stay near my lodge. Horses are a lot like children. They must be taught the proper way of doing things, and when they have been they usually turn out all right."

Nate admired the fine animals the warrior owned. He knew how highly Indians valued their horses, especially their war-horses, the mounts warriors invariably rode while raiding or hunting. Such steeds had to be fearless, fast, and responsive to the slightest pressure from the warriors. "Surely one must stray off every now and then," Nate said.

"Unfortunately, yes."

"What do you then? Beat it?"

Spotted Bull recoiled in shock. "I would never beat an animal. Such cruelty is unnecessary."

"Then what do you do when a horse won't behave?"

An impish grin curled the warrior's mouth. "I eat it." He turned and headed back.

Wondering if the Shoshone was joshing, Nate followed, tucking the Hawken in the crook of his left elbow. The women had gone inside. Approaching from the south was the same white-haired warrior who had supplied directions to the lodge.

"Here comes my friend, Lame Elk," Spotted Bull said.

"He told us where to find you," Nate said.

"Lame Elk and I have been on many hunts together. He saved me from a charging buffalo once. I had wounded it with my lance, and it turned on me and knocked my horse down before I could get away. I was pinned under my animal, helpless, and the buffalo moved in to gore me. That was when Lame Elk rode right up to it and buried his lance in the buffalo's chest."

"Friends like that are rare."

Spotted Bull glanced at him. "True, Grizzly Killer,

and worth more than the best war-horse that ever lived."

The elderly warrior reached them and was warmly greeted by Spotted Bull, who then made the formal introductions.

"It occurred to me who you must be after you had ridden off," Lame Elk said to Nate. "I have heard stories about you, and I thought I would come to learn if they are true."

"What kind of stories?" Nate asked.

"They say you are different from most whites, that you have the soul of an Indian in a white man's body. They say you kill grizzlies like most men kill ants. And they say you have slain more Blackfeet than anyone else," Lame Elk said.

"Whoever made these claims must have been hit on the head with a war club first," Nate joked.

Both Shoshones laughed.

"You are not vain," Lame Elk said. "That is good. There is too much vanity in the younger warriors these days. All they think of is wearing the best buckskin and riding the best horses. They must have a new lodge every year or so, even when their old one has not yet worn out. In my day things were different. A man was measured by his courage, not by his wealth. If a man had the smallest lodge in the village but was the bravest fighter in the tribe, he became a top man, maybe even a chief. Now a man would rather have twenty horses than have counted twenty coup, and those who have many possessions look down their noses at those who do not."

Spotted Bull grinned. "You exaggerate again, old friend."

"Do I?" Lame Elk asked.

Nate didn't think so. When first learning about Indian culture, he had been surprised that there actually were rich and poor Indians and that the gulf between them could be considerable. Certain chiefs and other wealthy warriors might own hundreds of horses, have two or three wives, and have a lodge large enough to accommodate 30 people at once. By contrast, there were warriors who only owned two or three horses, had one wife, and lived in a small lodge that threatened to fall over with the next strong gust of wind. In many respects Indians and whites were more alike than they realized or would admit. "If your people aren't careful, Lame Elk," he said, "they will become more and more like the whites until there is no difference between the two."

"If that ever happens, my people will deserve their fate," the elderly warrior said. "They will have lost the guidance of the Everywhere Spirit and be adrift in the world."

Nate detected melancholy in the old man's eyes. He thought about the reference to the Everywhere Spirit. Some Indians referred to God as the Great Medicine or Great Mystery. Others called the Supreme Deity the Great Spirit. All the terms meant the same thing, as far as he could determine. And he'd been amazed to discover how truly religious the Indians were. In their own way, Indians were generally even more spiritual than the majority of whites. Ironically, back in the States most folks regarded the Indians as heathens or pagans.

"Come inside and we will smoke the pipe," Spotted Bull said and stood aside to let them enter his lodge first.

Nate went in through the open flap. To his left, huddled together in animated conversation, were Winona, Willow Woman, and Morning Dove. Recalling the proper tepee etiquette, he stood to the right and waited for Spotted Bull to indicate where he should sit. As Shakespeare had told him, there were certain formal rules of conduct visitors to any lodge must follow. Not to do so was considered rude, an insult to the host.

The two men entered, and Spotted Bull asked that Nate sit in the seat of honor which was at the rear of the lodge and to the left of the spot where Spotted Bull normally took his seat. Lame Elk was asked to sit on Spotted Bull's right.

Nate leaned the Hawken against the wall, then sank down cross-legged as was the custom for Indian men. Women were strictly forbidden from doing so because they might inadvertently expose their upper legs or private parts; they must sit on their heels or kneel at all times when in mixed company.

"Bring my best pipe and the kinnikinnick," Spotted Bull said to his wife.

Morning Dove dutifully opened a parflache and took out an exquisitely adorned pipe and a buckskin pouch. She brought them over and placed them in front of her husband, then rejoined Winona and Willow Woman.

Nate got a good look at the pipe as Spotted Bull started filling the intricately carved buffalo-shaped bowl. Indians took great stock in their pipes. A fine one like his host's would be worth at least one horse or several buffalo robes in trade. It was decorated with brown horsehair, which hung over two dozen glass beads, four silk ribbons, and bands of wool. Nate figured it was Spotted Bull's best pipe, one reserved specifically for special occasions. Most warriors owned at least two: one for everyday use and one for ceremonial purposes.

Whichever pipe was used, smoking was considered a solemn ritual. Indians smoked to ratify personal pledges, to formalize agreements between tribes, to communicate with the spirit world, and to display a token of friendship. When a warrior invited someone into his lodge to smoke with him, it meant the warrior had only the friendliest of intentions and could be counted on to be as good as his word.

Spotted Bull wore an intent expression as he packed the mixture of tobacco and willow bark into the bowl. This mixture, known as kinnikinnick, varied from tribe to tribe and even between individuals. Because the wild tobacco Indians harvested was exceptionally strong, they often added other ingredients for balance. Bearberries, sumac leaves, and willow bark were all favorites.

Having tamped the contents of the bowl down to his satisfaction, Spotted Bull moved to the fire and retrieved a burning brand. He lit the kinnikinnick, puffing heavily as wreaths of smoke floated toward the ventilation opening at the top of the conical lodge. When at last he had the pipe going to his satisfaction, he took his seat and offered it to Nate. "Here, Grizzly Killer. As my guest of honor, you go first."

"Thank you," Nate said, taking the long pipe in both hands. He'd only smoked a few times, and he hoped he wouldn't embarrass himself by coughing or hacking. As he touched the stem to his lips, Spotted Bull made a comment that caused him to forget all about such a minor matter.

"There is something I would like to discuss with you as we smoke. How would you like to go on a surround with us?"

Chapter Seven

"After buffalo?" Nate asked, stunned by the proposal.

Lame Elk snickered. "We rarely surround rabbits," he said, his eyes twinkling.

"The hunt is still being planned," Spotted Bull said. "It might be four or five sleeps before the hunters leave. Would you like to go?"

Nate became aware of Winona staring at him. All the women had ceased chatting. He lowered the pipestem a fraction and tried to keep his voice steady as he answered. "Will the hunters be traveling all the way to the plains?"

"Yes," Spotted Bull confirmed. "The trip there for us will take about three sleeps. There is no telling how long the surround will take because there is no way of predicting how many buffalo will be slain and how long it will take to butcher them."

"Which means I would be away from my wife for quite a while," Nate observed.

"Is that a problem?" Spotted Bull asked and then glanced at Winona. A knowing smile brightened his face. "Oh. I am sorry. I almost forgot about the birth. This will be your first child, and a husband should be with his wife at such a time."

Relief washed over Nate. He had a legitimate excuse to bow out of the surround, and after all the terrible tales he'd heard about the practice he wasn't inclined to jeopardize his life with Winona due to deliver any day now. "I will give it some thought," he said, "but I will be honest and tell you that under the circumstances I believe my place is with Winona."

Lame Elk snorted. "Our young warriors do the same thing. They refuse to go hunting or raiding while their wives are heavy with child. Back in my time things were different. When a woman was ready to have a baby, she just walked into the woods, squatted, and out it dropped. She never made any fuss about it, and she never asked her husband to stay around and hold her hand."

"Behave yourself," Spotted Bull said and grinned at Nate. "You must overlook his words sometimes. In his advanced years he has become as testy as a rattlesnake."

"I have not," Lame Elk said. "All I'm doing is dispensing the wisdom of my years, and you should have the courtesy to listen without criticizing me."

Nate chuckled. He could tell the two friends enjoyed needling one another. "How many warriors will go on the surround?" he asked out of curiosity.

"Twenty-five or thirty," Spotted Bull said. "I will be leading them."

Morning Dove interjected a remark. "You need not go, husband. The younger warriors can manage quite well without you."

"We have already talked this over several times," Spotted Bull reminded her. "I have not been on a surround in many winters and I want to do it one more time."

"You can go off and kill a buffalo any time you want," Morning Dove said. "Leave the surrounds to the young men."

Spotted Bull frowned. "Why must you keep making an issue of my age? I can still ride with the best of them and shoot an arrow as straight as anyone in the village. My war-horse is experienced and quick on its feet. You need not concern yourself over my safety."

Although Nate felt inclined to agree with Morning Dove, he knew it would be considered bad manners if he were to involve himself in their personal dispute. The worry in her eyes was as plain as the nose on her face, and he didn't blame her one bit. Surrounds were too dangerous for a man of Spotted Bull's advanced years, and he wondered what the warrior was trying to prove by going on one.

"Excuse me, Grizzly Killer," Lame Elk said. "Are you planning to keep that pipe or will you smoke sometime today and let us share also?"

"Sorry," Nate said and self-consciously took a puff, drawing the smoke down into his lungs and then exhaling loudly. He suppressed a strong impulse to cough and handed the pipe back to his host.

Spotted Bull took the pipe without comment and gave it to Lame Elk, who smiled and puffed vigorously.

The women began conversing in low tones.

"So tell me," Spotted Bull said, looking at Nate, "did you happen to see any sign of Blackfeet on your way here?"

"No. Have there been any reported in this area?"

"Five sleeps ago a party of hunters came across signs that a small band of Blackfeet were roaming the country north of our village. Since then no one has seen a thing."

Bitter memories of Nate's previous conflicts with

the bloodthirsty Blackfeet filled his mind. Of all the tribes in the northern and central Rockies, the Blackfeet were the most feared and with good reason. They killed whites on sight and made relentless war on practically every other tribe. The Blackfeet exhibited the same unbridled ferocity as the Comanches, who dwelt far to the south, and the Apaches, who lived a great distance to the southwest. But of the three, the Blackfeet were widely regarded as the worst.

"I doubt a small band would dare bother a village this size," Spotted Bull was saying. "Even Blackfeet are not that crazy."

"There is no telling where they are concerned," Nate said.

"True, Grizzly Killer," Lame Elk interjected, exhaling a cloud of smoke. "The Blackfeet have always regarded themselves as the best fighters in existence. In order to prove this, all they do is fight, fight, fight. They don't care if they are outnumbered. And they are not afraid to die. Why, once when I was a boy I witnessed a battle between sixty of our warriors and twelve Blackfeet who came too near our camp and were spotted. Although the Blackfeet were surrounded, they formed into a wedge and attacked our warriors like rabid wolves. I was amazed by what I saw."

"Were all the Blackfeet slain?"

"Not at first. Five were only wounded," Lame Elk related. "Our men let the women beat on them for a while, and then our warriors gouged out their eyes, cut off their tongues and noses, and hacked their bodies into tiny bits. Other boys and I picked up some of the body parts and threw them at each other. Later the pieces were fed to the camp dogs." He smiled wistfully. "It was a grand time for everyone."

Nate glanced at Winona. Her parents had been

killed by Blackfeet, and he didn't want to upset her by discussing the Blackfeet further and possibly sparking sad recollections of the event. "Are there any other white men here?" he asked to change the topic.

"Three trappers visited us six sleeps ago," Spotted Bull answered. "They only stayed for one night and then went off to lay their traps for beaver."

Nate nodded. If not for the pregnancy, he would be out doing the same thing himself. The more pelts he could collect before the annual rendezvous, the more money and trade goods he would reap as his reward.

"One of the trappers told us there is a large Flathead village fifteen sleeps to the northwest of here," Spotted Bull said.

Right away Nate thought of his mentor, Shakespeare. The last time he'd seen McNair had been at a Flathead village where his friend had married a Flathead woman, Indian fashion. He wondered if Shakespeare was still there, or if the newlyweds had gone to Shakespeare's cabin, which was located not all that far from Nate's own. He decided to stop and see them on the way home.

"We are not very concerned about the Flatheads," Spotted Bull said. "They leave us alone and we leave them alone. Why should we waste energy fighting them when there are always plenty of Blackfeet and Utes to fight?"

"The Flatheads are fine people," Nate said. "I lived with them for a short while recently. They treated me courteously."

Lame Elk leaned forward to gaze at him. "I have heard that Flathead women are as beautiful as our own. Is this true?"

Suddenly Winona, Morning Dove, and Willow Woman stopped talking and fixed their attention on Nate, waiting expectantly to hear the answer he would give.

Resisting an urge to snicker, Nate said, "It's true the Flathead women are quite lovely, but they cannot begin to compare to Shoshone women. In all my travels I've never seen women anywhere who are as beautiful as yours."

"I thought as much," Lame Elk said.

All three women smiled and went back to talking.

"Grizzly Killer is wise beyond his years," Spotted Bull said softly, a grin touching his lips.

Nate moved his head a bit closer to his host and whispered, "Marriage does that to a man. I would rather face a horde of enraged Blackfeet than one angry wife."

Spotted Bull chuckled. "The Blackfeet would treat you better," he said.

Laughing, Nate nodded and bestowed a loving look on Winona when she gazed in his direction.

Lame Elk took another puff and said in all earnestness, "Women have always been a mystery to me. When I was a young man I thought I knew all there was to know about them. Then I took a beautiful woman as my wife and discovered everything I thought was wrong. So I changed my thinking and took a second woman into my lodge. It was most confusing. Everything I had learned from the first woman did little to help me understand the second woman." He paused, his forehead creased in deep contemplation. "Finally I decided men are not meant to understand women. I do not know why this should be unless the Everywhere Spirit has a strange sense of humor."

"Women are like the spirit realm," Spotted Bull said. "They are one of the two great mysteries in life."

Nate noticed that the women were staring at them again so he promptly changed the subject. "Does every Shoshone believe in the Everywhere Spirit?"

Spotted Bull and Lame Elk glanced at him. "Of

course," the former said. "Why do you ask?"

"Because a while ago I was thinking about the fact that Indian people as a whole are more spiritual than my own people," Nate said.

"I have noticed this," Lame Elk said. "White people do not seem to know about spirit things. They do not let the Everywhere Spirit guide their lives. They do not even know they have a spirit center. This, too, is most perplexing. I do not see how the whites can hope to prosper unless they drastically change their ways."

"I am sorry to say it, but I agree," Spotted Bull said to Nate. "Your people are more puzzling than women. Whites treat the land as if they own it, and they take more from the land than they give to it. This is terribly wrong." He scratched his chin. "Look at what has happened to the beaver. In the few winters that white trappers have been taking pelts, more beavers have been killed than in all the winters that have gone before all the way back to the beginning of all things. Why do whites have such little regard for the natural order of the world?"

"I honestly do not know," Nate replied.

"Well I do," Lame Elk said. "I have given the matter much thought and I believe the problem is that whites do not go around barefoot enough."

Nate blinked, uncertain if he'd heard correctly. "I don't follow you."

"I was told that most white men wear heavy boots and white women wear odd shoes all the time. The trappers and a few others wear moccasins. But except for white children, hardly any whites ever go around barefoot," Lame Elk said. "How do your people expect to stay in touch with Nature if they fail to take a walk in the grass every now and then? We must feel the earth under our naked feet if we are to fully appreciate our ties to the natural order of things."

"I never thought of it in quite that way," Nate said.

Just then, from off to the south, arose the clamor of many voices and the sound of a general commotion. Footsteps pounded outside the lodge entrance and a male voice called out, "Spotted Bull, this is Fox Tail. May I speak to you?"

"Enter," Spotted Bull said.

A young warrior poked his head inside. "I thought you would like to know. A hunting party has just returned, and they have captured an enemy of our people."

"Where are they now?" Spotted Bull asked, rising.

"On the south shore of the lake near Chief Broken Paw's lodge," the young warrior said. "Now, if you will excuse me, I must inform others."

"Thank you for telling us," Spotted Bull said.

The young warrior backed out and raced off.

"This is great news," Lame Elk said. "Things were getting too boring around here. Now we will have some excitement. Maybe we will get to torture this enemy before he dies." He laid down the pipe and pushed himself up to his feet. "Let us go see what is happening."

Spotted Bull looked at Nate. "Would you like to come along?"

"I certainly would," Nate said, rising and grabbing the Hawken. He winked at Winona and trailed the two men outside where the bright light made him squint. They turned southward, joining scores of other Shoshones, mostly men but also a few women who had heard the news and were eager to glimpse the prisoner for themselves.

By the time Nate and his new friends arrived at the chief's huge lodge, over 100 Shoshones already ringed the lodge entrance where the chief, the hunting party, and the captive now stood. Nate had to stand on tiptoe to see the members of the hunting party, and he was surprised to spot Drags The Rope among them. Then the ranks of spectators in front of him momentarily parted and he got a good look at the prisoner. His blood ran cold at the sight.

It was Red Hawk.

Chapter Eight

The Dakota warrior stood with his shoulders squared and his head held erect and proud, radiating defiance from every pore. His wrists had been bound with thick strips of leather behind his back. His chest and arms bore scratch marks, indicating he had been involved in a fight, and a jagged tear now marred his leggings from his left knee to his ankle. All of his weapons had been confiscated. His brown stallion was off to the left with the mounts belonging to the hunting party.

Drags The Rope was engaged in earnest conversation with an elderly warrior who wore a crown of eagle feathers.

Some of the Shoshones were taunting the Sioux, insulting his tribe and lineage or casting aspersions on his manhood. A few bold children dashed up to him and threw sticks at his face and torso.

Nate didn't know what to do. During the brief time he'd been with Red Hawk, he'd grown to like him. He didn't want to see anything happen to the outcast. But he worried that if he dared to speak up the Shoshones might hold it against him. He bided his time and moved closer, trying to hear the discussion between Drags The Rope and Chief Broken Paw.

"—climbed a ridge to spot game and saw him watering his horse at a stream," Drags The Rope was saying. "White Lynx, Man Afraid, and I sneaked down and surprised him while he was seated on the bank, deep in thought. He never heard us coming. Once we laid our hands on him, he put up a great struggle. The others had to come help us subdue him."

The Chief glanced at their prisoner. "I know you are an Oglala. Do you speak our tongue?"

Red Hawk made no reply.

"Very well," Broken Paw said and switched to sign language. "We will untie you so you can speak in sign. If you try to get away, we will cut your feet off." He nodded at Drags The Rope.

A knife flashed in the sunlight and the leather strips binding the Sioux fell to the grass. He began rubbing his wrists while glaring at his captors.

"Now tell us your name," Broken Paw said.

"Red Hawk."

"Where is the rest of your war party? Were you sent ahead to spy on our village? How many Dakotas are with you?" Broken Paw asked, his hands flying.

"I am alone."

The chief frowned. "Do you take me for a fool, Oglala? You would have me believe that you came all the way from the Dakota hunting grounds alone?"

"I speak the truth," Red Hawk said. "I am not here on a raid. All I want is to be left in peace."

Many in the crowd started whispering, and from the baleful glances they cast at the captive it became apparent to Nate that Red Hawk would be extremely lucky to live out the hour.

A husky Shoshone standing near Drags The Rope

suddenly raised a war club overhead and bellowed for all to hear. "There is only one way to deal with this Oglala dog! I say we treat him as his kind would treat us!"

There were cries of assent from a number of spectators, and a few men clamored for the Sioux's scalp.

Nate realized the Shoshones were gradually working themselves into a killing frame of mind. No matter what Red Hawk said, the Shoshones wouldn't believe him. He hefted the Hawken, debating what to do. As an adopted member of the tribe he was welcome to speak up at formal gatherings, but he didn't know what to say.

Broken Paw gestured for silence and faced the prisoner again. "If you are not here on a raid, then why are you in our territory?"

"I am passing through," Red Hawk said. "I did not know I was close to your village until a short while before your warriors jumped me, and I was heading away from here when they did."

"Even if your words are true," Broken Paw signed, "our people and yours have fought a number of times in the past. We have no treaty with the Oglalas. This makes you our enemy."

Red Hawk sighed. "I know."

"As our enemy, you know the treatment you will receive," Broken Paw said. "The same treatment your people would give one of us if the situation was reversed."

Suddenly the husky warrior gave Red Hawk a brutal shove that knocked the Dakota to his knees, then waved his war club in the air and whooped wildly. "I say we stake this dog out and try our luck with lances."

"I agree, White Lynx!" one of the watching warriors called out. "He will look like a porcupine when we are done."

Nate glanced at Spotted Bull and Lame Elk, both of

whom were solemnly observing the proceedings. He doubted either would help him if he dared to intervene.

White Lynx took hold of Red Hawk's hair and jerked savagely. "Who will help me stake him out?"

Several men eagerly started forward.

Horrified at the prospect of Red Hawk being killed, Nate gripped the Hawken in both hands and gulped. It was now or never. He might not be able to influence the outcome, but at least he could live with his conscience if he knew he'd tried his best to assist the Dakota. His every nerve tingling, he took several strides past the ring of Shoshones and shouted at the top of his lungs. "No!"

Total silence abruptly engulfed the Shoshones. Amazed expressions were turned in the frontiersman's direction and a murmur rippled among the crowd.

Broken Paw pivoted, betraying surprise when he laid eyes on Nate. "And who are you, white man? I do not believe we have ever met."

"I am known as Grizzly Killer," Nate said formally. "I am married to Black Kettle's daughter, Winona." He became aware that Spotted Bull and Lame Elk were standing at his side.

"Yes. I have heard of you," Broken Paw said, stepping forward. He gestured at Red Hawk. "Why do you seek to protect this man?"

"I know him," Nate declared and listened to even more whispering break out among the spectators.

"How is this possible?" Broken Paw asked in surprise.

"My wife and I met him earlier. He saved us from a grizzly," Nate said and launched into a brief recital of the encounter. He concluded his story by saying, "You should believe him when he says he is alone. He is an outcast."

"Oh?" Broken Paw said, glancing at the captive, his

eyebrows arched. "That would explain a lot."

"He made no attempt to harm us," Nate said, hoping to convince the chief to spare the Dakota's life. "Yet had he wanted to, he could easily have ambushed us."

White Lynx let go of Red Hawk's long hair and stalked toward Nate. "What difference does that make, white eyes? The Oglala is still our enemy and everyone knows what we must do to him."

"Why not let him live?" Nate asked.

"So that he might sneak back here in the dead of night and murder some of us in our sleep?" White Lynx rejoined in contempt. "No. I say we kill him now."

"It is customary for us to slay enemies of our people," Broken Paw agreed. "If we were to let this one go, it would show us to be weak."

"Not at all," Nate said. "It would show that you have wisdom and compassion. The true mark of a warrior is knowing when to kill and when not to kill."

"What do you know about being a warrior, white man?" White Lynx asked.

"My name is Grizzly Killer," Nate said.

"So I have heard, but it does not impress me as it does so many others," White Lynx said. "To me you are nothing but a white man, and a white man has no business interfering in tribal matters."

"That is no way to talk," Broken Paw said. "You know that Grizzly Killer has every right to speak as he wishes. By taking Winona as his wife, he has become a part of our tribe."

White Lynx sneered. "Next we will be admitting Blackfeet and Kiowas." He jabbed a thumb at Nate while addressing the chief. "What does he know of our ways? No matter what you say, he is not a Shoshone."

"I can speak for myself," Nate said before Broken

Paw could answer. "It's true I wasn't born into the tribe, but I admire and respect the Shoshone way of living more than I do the way of the white man. My heart is the heart of an Indian."

A snort burst from White Lynx. "You are touched in the head, white man. Only an Indian knows the heart of an Indian."

Nate's anger flared. He'd tolerated all of the insults and belligerence he could stomach. "And only a fool takes a human life, white or Indian, without just cause. To kill the Dakota just because he is from a different tribe is something the Blackfeet would do, and I thought the Shoshones were better than the Blackfeet."

White Lynx bristled, hefting his war club. "Are you calling me a fool?"

Broken Paw looked from one to the other. "Enough of this bickering," he said sternly. "We should behave as reasonable men."

"What is there to be reasonable about?" White Lynx demanded. "I say we kill the Dakota now. Let Grizzly Killer go hide in a lodge if he is afraid to watch."

Struggling to restrain himself, Nate said, "And I say killing the Dakota is bad medicine. Spare him instead."

"Both of you have good points," Broken Paw said diplomatically. "This is a grave issue that should not be decided by one man alone. We will call a council and discuss what is best to do."

"A council? Why waste the time over such a trifle?" White Lynx asked.

"Since when is the taking of any life a trifle?" Broken Paw said. "No, we will let the Dakota live until after we hold a council tonight."

"Then let me have him until then," White Lynx said, leering. "I will give him the treatment he deserves."

The chief hesitated, then said emphatically, "No. The Oglala will be in Grizzly Killer's custody until after the council meeting."

"You pick this white eyes over me?" White Lynx snapped.

Unruffled, Broken Paw said, "Grizzly Killer is the one who has spoken in the Oglala's defense. It is only fitting that he look after the prisoner."

White Lynx glared at Nate. "I will remember this," he said and abruptly stormed off into the crowd, shouldering his way through, oblivious to the reproach of those he bumped aside.

Nate was elated at the temporary reprieve he'd obtained for the Sioux. He motioned for Red Hawk to join him.

"While I admire what you have done," Broken Paw said, "and might even agree with you, there is something you should know."

"What?"

"You are responsible for this man," Broken Paw said. "If he escapes, you will be punished. If he kills or hurts anyone, you will be held accountable. Your fate is as much in his hands as his is in yours." He paused. "Are you certain you want to go through with this?"

Red Hawk reached them and halted. He gave Nate a grateful smile.

"I'm certain," Nate said.

"Very well. Just remember you have been warned," Broken Paw said and walked toward his lodge.

Now that the issue had been decided, the hunting party and the spectators began to disperse. Many conversed in low tones.

Nate watched them go. Within an hour the argument would be the talk of the tribe. He looked at Spotted Bull, who was staring at him strangely. "With your permission, I will keep Red Hawk in your lodge until tonight. I promise to keep an eye on him the whole time."

"It is against my better judgment, but I trust you," Spotted Bull said. "Very well. This Oglala may stay with us. I will go on ahead and inform the women so it doesn't come as a shock." He moved off, Lame Elk at his side.

Nate drew his knife, stepped behind the Dakota, and carefully sliced the leather strips in half. When they fell to the ground he slid the knife back into its sheath and tucked the Hawken under his left arm to leave his hands free for signing.

Red Hawk turned. "Thank you, Grizzly Killer, for speaking in my behalf."

"Perhaps one day you can return the favor," Nate signed and started toward Spotted Bull's lodge. "Come with me." He was conscious of the stares of the Shoshones who had not yet left, a few openly hostile. Not everyone agreed with Broken Paw's decision.

"As much as I would like to do you a kindness," Red Hawk signed, "I doubt I will live long enough to be able to pay you back."

"You do not know that for certain. There is to be a council. White Lynx might not get his way. The council meeting will be conducted by the older warriors and they are not as bloodthirsty as he is."

"I hope you are right," Red Hawk said. "Although there have been many times since I became an outcast that I wished I were dead, now that I face the prospect I find death is not so appealing any more."

Nate glanced at the Dakota, curiosity eating at him. "Do you mind if I ask you a personal question?" he signed.

"I can imagine what it is."

"If you think I am prying into your personal affairs, I won't insist on an answer."

Red Hawk sighed, then moved his hands slowly. "You want to ask me the reason my people cast me out."

"If you care to tell me."

"After what you have done for me, it is only fitting that you know," Red Hawk said, a melancholy shadow darkening his features. "I am an outcast because I murdered an unarmed member of my tribe."

Chapter Nine

The revelation upset Nate although it came as no great surprise. Banishment from a tribe was a severe practice adopted as a last resort. Only the gravest of offenses could result in a warrior being made an outcast. It was rarely done. He knew of only two other instances, and both of those, like this one, involved murder.

The truth of the matter was that Indians seldom killed fellow tribal members. They would go off and raid another tribe and kill with reckless abandon, but once back in their own village they were expected to keep a lid on their tempers no matter what the provocation might be.

All tribes preferred to settle personal disputes in a civil matter. The Indians dwelling on the plains east of the Rockies even had what were known as soldier societies who policed the encampments and punished those who broke tribal custom. Violators would be judged according to the seriousness of the offense, the reason for the violation, and the culprit's attitude. Punishments ranged from light, such as having an ear cut off the offender's war-horse, to severe, such as beating the offender so badly he could barely stand.

Knowing all this, Nate had surmised that Red Hawk's offense must have been extreme, but he hadn't pegged the Dakota as a wanton murderer. And now, looking into the warrior's troubled eyes and recalling how Red Hawk had deliberately risked his life to save Winona and him from the grizzly bear, Nate figured there must be more to the story. "Want to talk about it?" he asked.

"There is nothing to say. I was guilty. My punishment was just."

Nate reluctantly decided to drop the subject. Further questions would be a rude breach of Indian etiquette and might offend Red Hawk. He heard voices upraised in anger and looked up to see Spotted Bull and White Lynx arguing. Lame Elk stood to one side, while behind White Lynx were two other warriors.

"—none of your concern," Spotted Bull was saying. "And I will not stand by and let you insult him."

"I never thought you would side with a white man against your own people," White Lynx said.

Nate was almost to them. Suddenly one of the other warriors saw him and whispered a word in warning to White Lynx, who looked over Spotted Bull's shoulder and smirked.

"And here he is now. We were just talking about you."

"So I gathered," Nate said coldly. "If you have something to say about me, say it to my face." He paused. "That is, if you are man enough."

White Lynx flushed scarlet and glowered. "No one can accuse me of being a coward. I have counted twelve coup, two on Blackfeet. Ten scalps hang in my lodge. And I have led five successful raids."

Despite himself, Nate was impressed. Twelve coup was quite a feat, above average for a man White Lynx's age. Even more remarkable were the five successful raids. It meant that the raiding parties had not lost a single warrior, and losses of one or two men on a raid were not uncommon. White Lynx, therefore, for all his fiery temperament, was a competent, brave warrior who must enjoy considerable esteem in his tribe. Nate kept his features composed and said, "Then tell me what you were talking about."

"I was telling Spotted Bull that he makes a mistake in letting you stay with him," White Lynx said. "Even though you took one of our women for your wife, you do not have the best interests of our people at heart. You are like some other white men I have known. You think you know better than we do how we should live our lives."

Nate was about to protest when he realized that the Shoshone, in a sense, was right. He'd known his fair share of trappers and traders who tended to look down their noses at the Indians and regarded all tribes with paternal contempt. There were many whites with very firm and drastic opinions on how to deal with the Indians, not the least of whom was President Andrew Jackson. "Old Hickory"—as Jackson was widely known because he had been as tough as hickory during his illustrious military career—felt it was the inalienable right of the federal government to do whatever might be necessary to subjugate the Indian tribes and force the Indians to live wherever the government saw fit to place them. Already thousands of Indians had been compelled to move west of the Mississippi, with countless numbers dying along the way. In the midst of his thoughts, Nate suddenly realized over half a minute had gone by and the Shoshones were regarding him expectantly.

"Why do you not speak?" White Lynx asked.

"I was thinking about your words," Nate said. "And I agree with you to a point."

"You do?" White Lynx said in surprise.

"Yes. Many whites do believe they know more about things than your people do," Nate said, "but I have learned they are wrong. And the reason I objected to killing Red Hawk has nothing to do with such an attitude. I do not think any life should be taken lightly, even the life of an enemy. The man who does so is no better than the bear I have been named after."

The speech appeared to have a positive impact on the two warriors with White Lynx. They exchanged looks and one of them said softly, "His words are true, I think."

White Lynx cocked his head and examined Nate as if under a microscope. "Perhaps I have misjudged you a little, but I still feel we are making a mistake by not killing this Oglala right away. And tonight I will argue at the council to have him put to death."

"What if the council decides against you?" Nate asked.

"Then I will abide by their wishes," White Lynx said, his tone implying he would rather not. He abruptly turned around and walked off without another word, his friends in tow.

Nate looked at Spotted Bull. "I am sorry for any problems this will cause you."

"There may be a few like White Lynx who will think badly of me for a time, but most of the tribe will understand," Spotted Bull said, leading the way northward.

"I hope so," Nate replied. He glanced at Red Hawk to make certain the Sioux was following, then surveyed the encampment. The situation accented his odd feeling of being an outsider, and he began to wish he'd stayed back in the cabin. Then he thought of Winona. "I forgot to bring this up earlier, but I have been told that your tribe uses midwives to assist women in having babies."

"This is so," Spotted Bull said.

"Can you recommend a good one?" Nate asked. Behind him Lame Elk gave a little laugh.

"Your wife can pick a midwife on her own. Having babies is something women do very well. Men should not concern themselves with such matters."

"I am concerned for Winona's safety and health," Nate said defensively. "What is wrong with that?"

"You have much to learn about men and women," Lame Elk said. "There are certain things only women are meant to do and other things only men are meant to do. Since there has never been a single man who has given birth, so far as I am aware, it is best for men to let women take care of dropping babies. They know how to do it. We do not. It is as simple as that, and that is why it is unwise for a man to meddle in the affairs of women and for women to meddle in our affairs."

Spotted Bull chuckled. "You are talking in circles again."

"No, you are listening in circles," the elderly Shoshone said.

Nate was about to press for more information on the midwives when a shriek of sheer terror sounded to the east. Immediately Spotted Bull turned and ran to investigate. "Come," Nate signed to Red Hawk and followed.

Other Shoshones were hastening toward the person who had screamed, a young woman standing at the very edge of the encampment with her face buried in her hands. She sobbed hysterically.

Nate slowed as he neared her. Several women and men were already there, trying to comfort her and asking about the reason for the scream. They spoke swiftly, almost too fast for Nate to understand. Then the terrified woman answered, and he was able to get the gist of her statement.

Her child had been crying, and to teach it a lesson she had taken the infant out past the last row of lodges in the village and hung the child's cradleboard on a bush. This was a widespread Indian custom. Crying was not permitted because the wailing could give away the position of a camp to enemies who might be in the area. Consequently, when babies cried too long or too loud they were taken out and hidden in the brush. When the infants calmed down, their mothers retrieved them. It seldom took more than two or three times for even the most stubborn child to learn that crying wasn't tolerated and to refrain from doing so.

Now this woman had done the same thing, but when she heard her baby stop wailing and went to get it, the child and the cradleboard were gone and imprinted in the soil near the bush were the large tracks of a mountain lion.

As the distraught mother concluded her narrative, warriors hastened off to grab their weapons and other women tried to comfort her.

Nate saw Spotted Bull race away, then faced eastward. He already had his Hawken. If he hurried, he'd reach the scene first and possibly find the big cat if it was still in the area, before a group of excited warriors arrived to scare it off. He broke into a run, the rifle clutched in his right hand, and quickly left the crowd behind. Winding among the lodges, he soon came to the perimeter. Only then did he become aware of the soft pad of footsteps to his rear, and he stopped to look over his left shoulder.

Red Hawk was trailing along, ten feet back.

"Stay here," Nate signed. "A mountain lion has taken a child and I must try to save it."

The Oglala halted and scanned the terrain ahead. "I will stay with you," he signed.

"But you are unarmed."

"I will not stay in the village without you," Red Hawk said. "What does it matter whether I face a mountain lion or White Lynx?"

Reluctantly, Nate resumed running. Had there been more time he would have argued the point, but every second wasted now was crucial. There was a slim chance the infant was still alive. Mountain lions often took their prey into thickets or crevasses where the meat could be consumed in peace and quiet, and if he could locate the cat swiftly then the baby stood a chance. If not, he didn't like to think about the consequences.

A narrow field bordered the village on the east. Beyond the field lay rugged woodland.

As Nate sprinted across the field he spied a tall bush off to the left, beside a small boulder. The bush had thick limbs, ideal for supporting a cradleboard. On a hunch he ran to the bush and examined the ground around it, but he saw nothing until Red Hawk gave his arm a nudge.

The Sioux pointed at a circle of barren earth next to his moccasins.

Goose bumps broke out over Nate's skin as he laid eyes on the immense paw print. He'd seen panther tracks before, distinctive by their large size, their four toes, and a complete absence of claw marks. In this case the print measured approximately four inches in length and four-and-a-half inches in width, exceptionally big even for a mountain lion. He guessed that the print was of a front foot because the front feet were normally larger than the rear feet. Even so, they were after a giant feline.

Red Hawk pointed to the southeast, the direction the print was slanted, and led the way.

Nate was about to object, but changed his mind. Undoubtedly the Oglala was a much better tracker. He would rely on Red Hawk's skill and stay alert enough to protect his newfound friend should they run into trouble.

They entered the forest and found more tracks in a small clearing. Red Hawk picked up the pace, reading the signs faster than seemed humanly possible. Predictably, the big cat had stuck to the open ground in its haste to put distance between itself and the village.

Nate constantly scoured the vegetation before them, hoping to glimpse the predator and its tiny burden. Since they had not found the cradleboard yet, he figured the panther must have the board in its mouth. An image of the cat's long teeth impaling the infant brought a shudder to his spine, and he shook his head to dispel it.

Cradleboards were universally used by Indians. Consisting essentially of a wooden frame over which a soft pouch was sewn, the ingenuous device was used to transport an infant everywhere. It could be slung on the mother's back, hung on a horse, strapped to a travois, or simply carried when the tribe was on the march. And when not being used to convey the baby, the cradleboard could be leaned against any convenient support, such as the wall of a lodge. At all times the baby was kept upright. The cradleboards varied widely in size and construction. Those of wealthy parents were often gaily painted and adorned with beads or horse hair. Those owned by poorer parents usually were little more than a bare skin stretched over the wood frame.

Nate realized the prints were leading toward a dense thicket, and he hoped the cat might be within the tangle of vegetation. Instead, the tracks skirted the thicket on the right and continued southeastward, perhaps in the direction of the mountain lion's den. Doubt assailed him, and he wondered if they were wasting their time, if the lion was already feasting on the child.

Then, from not more than a dozen yards in front of them, there came a low, raspy snarl.

Chapter Ten

The dense undergrowth prevented Nate from spotting the big cat. He tucked the Hawken to his shoulder to be ready in case it should charge out at them and quickly stepped abreast of Red Hawk to be in a better position to defend him. The trees ahead thinned out, and there appeared to be a clearing on the other side of a wide strip of waist-high weeds. Maybe, he reasoned, the mountain lion had stopped there to eat.

Red Hawk motioned for Nate to stop and went to move into the weeds.

Nate gripped the Oglala's arm and held him in place. When Red Hawk looked at him questioningly, he used one hand to indicate he was going to take the lead. With his other hand, Nate parted the weeds quietly, his nerves on the raw edge, his eyes darting right and left. Seven yards into the strip he noticed a break in the vegetation a few more yards in front of him. Puzzled, he warily stepped forward until he could see that the break was actually a drop-off, the top of an earthen bank that blocked from his view whatever lay below.

Exercising extreme caution, Nate moved closer to the rim of the bank. He heard a guttural cough, then the distinct whine of an infant. The baby was down there! Eager to save the child, he dashed forward and took in the scene 12 feet below.

The mountain lion stood in the middle of a secluded gully. At its huge feet rested the cradleboard, and the child inside was crying softly and waving its arms about, its small fingers jutting out of the opening at the top. The lion was eyeing the baby hungrily and might tear into it at any moment.

Nate took a hasty bead on the cat's head, hoping to end the menace with one shot, but in his eagerness he took another half step forward to be sure of not missing. He began to steady his rifle when he felt his left foot slip out from under him. Startled, he realized he was going over the bank, and the next second he plummeted feet first toward the ground below. Although Nate fell only 12 feet, the landing jarred his feet and legs, pitching him off balance so that he wound up on his stinging knees, the rifle clutched firmly in both hands. The cougar crouched and regarded him coldly.

He started to bring the Hawken to bear again when the big cat suddenly came toward him, walking slowly, its pads making no noise whatsoever. Only six feet separated them, and at such close range, staring into the depths of the mountain lion's eerie, slanted eyes, he froze. He wanted to shoot, to slay the beast, but try as he might his mind refused to function, refused to relay the mental message to his arms and hands.

The mountain lion came within two feet and halted. It regarded him intently, as if trying to make up its mind whether he qualified as dinner.

Now that the cat was so close, Nate couldn't fully extend the rifle to fire. He would have to level the gun from the waist and shoot. At such short range the odds of missing were remote, which bolstered his confidence. He girded himself, then swept into motion, whipping the Hawken barrel up as his thumb cocked the hammer. In the blink of an eye the muzzle was trained on the panther and his finger curled around the trigger. The blast caused the powerful rifle to buck in his hands and discharged a small cloud of gunsmoke.

Unfortunately, at the very instant he fired, the mountain lion leaped to one side, perhaps goaded by a primordial instinct that told it the gun was dangerous. The ball missed by a fraction and the lion vented an enraged roar, then pounced.

Nate was knocked onto his back by the heavy beast, the Hawken wedged between them. Inadvertently, the rifle saved his life, because the first swipe of the cat's razor-tipped claws was accidentally deflected by the Hawken. The panther snapped at Nate's face, and he narrowly evaded its raking teeth by twisting his head to the right. Frantic, he heaved, striving to throw the creature off him, but the huge lion weighed upwards of 300 pounds and it barely budged despite Nate's efforts. A paw struck his left shoulder a glancing blow, ripping open his buckskin shirt and slicing into his soft flesh. He squirmed and thrashed in a desperate bid for freedom, staring into the glaring orbs of his feline adversary, orbs that promised imminent death.

Unexpectedly, there came a whoop and something hit the mountain lion's left side. The cat bounded off Nate and whirled, temporarily forgetting about him to confront another attacker.

Nate scrambled to his feet, astounded to see Red Hawk beside the cradleboard, rocks held in each hand. He realized the Oglala had saved his life by throwing a rock at the panther, and he hoped to return the favor before the mountain lion sprang. Letting the rifle fall, he grabbed at his twin flintlocks, a hand closing on each one. But he was too late.

The cat hissed and leaped.

Red Hawk hurled both stones simultaneously even as he ducked low. Struck in the face, the mountain lion involuntarily jerked to the right, ruining the angle of its jump. It landed a yard shy of its intended victim and crouched, snarling savagely.

Nate wanted to shoot but couldn't. The cat was between Red Hawk and him, and there was the chance a ball would pass completely through the feline and hit the Sioux—or worse, the child. So he darted to the left to get a better shot.

Red Hawk was also in motion. He pivoted, clutched the cradleboard to his chest, and took off for the opposite side of the gully.

The lion roared and began to pursue him.

Finally Nate had the angle he wanted. He brought both flintlocks up, the hammers clicking as he cocked them, and squeezed both triggers at the same time. The smoothbore single-shot .55 caliber guns boomed louder than any rifle.

Two balls caught the big cat behind the left shoulder and bored deep into its body. It went down, rolling over and over, growling horribly, then stood upright with its face distorted in feral hatred. Blood oozed from the wounds, staining the beast's tawny hide a dark crimson.

Red Hawk reached the sheer gully wall and paused, seeking a way out. The child bawled in abject fright.

The mountain lion moved toward the Oglala and the baby.

There was no time for Nate to reload his pistols; he tossed them aside and drew his butcher knife, then ran to intercept the panther. A knife was no match for the cat's claws, but he would rather sell his life dearly than let the predator slay the infant. He vented a whoop that would have done justice to the fiercest Blackfoot who ever lived, trying to draw the cat's attention.

But the mountain lion ignored him. Instead, it crouched and coiled its mighty muscles for another leap at Red Hawk.

"No!" Nate shouted, afraid all his effort would be in vain. Then, from his rear, arose a series of low twangs, one after the other, at least a dozen in swift succession, and he heard a buzzing noise as slender shafts streaked past him to thud into the panther.

One moment the big cat was about to spring. The next, a dozen shafts protruded from its body and it was flipping wildly about, trying to tear out the offending arrows. It succeeded in breaking off two of them, but was unable to remove the barbed points imbedded in its sleek form. In a berserk fury it became a whirlwind of motion until, abruptly, it stiffened, vented a scream that sounded remarkably like that of a terrified woman, and collapsed on its side.

Yells of delight broke out behind Nate, and he turned to find over 20 Shoshone warriors spread out along the top of the earthen bank. Prominent among them were Spotted Bull and White Lynx, both holding bows. The warriors were all smiles, and those who had shot arrows were being clapped on the back and congratulated for a job well done. Nate slid his knife into its sheath, then faced the Oglala.

Red Hawk was walking toward him, the cradleboard nestled snugly in the crook of his left arm.

"Is the child all right?" Nate signed.

The Oglala held out the cradleboard so Nate could see for himself that the infant was unharmed and had stopped crying. There were teeth marks in the top of the cradleboard above the baby's hair, where the wood frame flared out to serve as a wide backrest for the child's head. Apparently the mountain lion had bitten into the cradleboard at just that one spot, its teeth missing the infant by less than an inch, when it carried the child to the gully.

Up close, Nate realized the baby was a little girl. He smiled and touched his finger to the child's cheek. She grinned, demonstrating the innate resilience of children to bounce back quickly from emotional distress. Where a minute earlier she had been crying, she now cooed happily. It made him think of the child Winona would soon deliver, and he longed to hold his own son or daughter in his arms.

"Is the baby hurt?" Spotted Bull called down.

Nate glanced around and shook his head out of force of habit. "No," he said. "She's fine, thanks to Red Hawk."

"I know," Spotted Bull said and bestowed a friendly smile on the Oglala. "We saw what he did."

Several of the warriors were moving south along the top of the gully, seeking an easy way down. They found a spot a dozen yards to the south where part of the bank had buckled, creating a gradual incline to the bottom. Yelling to the others, they descended.

Nate retrieved his pistols and wedged them under his belt. He was bending to pick up the Hawken when the Shoshones swarmed around him and Red Hawk, boisterously expressing their gratitude for saving the infant's life.

Suddenly White Lynx stepped in front of the Sioux and everyone else fell silent. He slung the bow over his left shoulder and coughed.

Red Hawk stood his ground, his features composed, the baby resting quietly in his arm.

Nate stared at the stocky Shoshone, wishing his guns were loaded. He wouldn't put it past White Lynx to start more trouble, and he wasn't about to let the man harass Red Hawk after what the Oglala had done.

"I arrived in time to see you try to save the child," White Lynx signed. He reached out, placed his right hand on Red Hawk's shoulder for a moment, and signed, "You are a good man, Dakota. I was wrong about you. Tonight I will say as much to the council and tell them of your deed."

Everyone else visibly relaxed.

White Lynx took Red Hawk by the arm and started to usher him from the gully when a lean warrior bounded up to the group and shoved his way through to the center. He was out of breath, his expression one of intense anxiety.

"My daughter?" he said.

Even though Red Hawk couldn't understand the words, he took one look at the man's face and extended the cradleboard toward him.

The newcomer took it and stared lovingly at the child. "You are safe," he said softly, almost choking on the words.

"Grizzly Killer and the Dakota saved her," White Lynx said. "Where were you, Tall Grass, when your daughter needed you the most?"

"I went to visit a friend on the other side of the village," the father said, leaning down to touch his nose to the little girl's. "I came as soon as someone told me."

"You should go show Clay Woman that your child is fine," Spotted Bull said. "She will be worried sick until you do."

"Yes, you are right," Tall Grass said absently and began to leave. He paused and gazed at Nate and Red Hawk. "Thank you," he said and his eyes brimmed with moisture. "I am forever in your debt." Then he spun around and hastened off.

The rest of the Shoshones started back. Four of them

picked up the mountain lion and brought up the rear. Nate fell in beside Red Hawk.

"It was too bad your clever trick did not work," the Dakota signed as they went up the incline.

"What trick was that?" Nate asked.

"I saw how you let the mountain lion get so close that you could not miss. I thought for sure you would kill it, but they can be very fast when they want to be."

"I noticed," Nate signed. He debated whether to admit the truth, to inform Red Hawk that he had frozen at a crucial moment, but decided against doing so. It was a personal matter, and he would deal with it in his own good time. Freezing when confronted with danger was not an uncommon experience. Any man might do so at one time or another. But if he did it again, if he found himself succumbing to inordinate fear on a regular basis, then he would have cause to worry greatly.

A large crowd of men, women, and children awaited the return of those who had hastened out to rescue the infant. The father became the center of attention as he and the mother tenderly clasped the child and received the heartfelt sympathies of their many friends and acquaintances. Averting the tragedy had put everyone in a good mood.

Nate received countless compliments, as did Red Hawk. Word of their battle with the mountain lion spread rapidly among the Shoshones, embellished, no doubt, in the telling, and Nate started to feel slightly embarrassed by the unwarranted attention. In one respect, though, he was delighted. Red Hawk had become the toast of the tribe, and not one Shoshone so much as gave him a hostile stare. It gave Nate cause to hope that all talk of killing the Sioux had died with the mountain lion.

After 20 minutes the Shoshones began to disperse. Spotted Bull led Nate and Red Hawk toward his lodge.

They covered only 30 yards when they saw Willow Woman hurrying in their direction.

"Grizzly Killer! You must come quickly!"

Alarmed, thinking that something must have happened to Winona or the baby, Nate ran to meet the young woman. "What is it?" he asked urgently.

"It is your wife. She is about to give birth."

Chapter Eleven

Give birth? Nate shook his head and said, "You must be mistaken. I left Winona a little while ago and she was fine. And the baby isn't due for fifteen sleeps or so yet."

"She is ready to have it now," Willow Woman said. "She sent me to find you because she knows you want to be with her when it happens."

Nate gazed northward in amazement, stunned by the realization that the blessed event he had been acutely dreading might actually be upon him.

"Sometimes babies drop early," Willow Woman said and motioned for him to get going. "Hurry. She can not hold it in forever."

"Hold it in?" Nate said and took off for the lodge as if a slavering grizzly was on his heels. In his mind's eye he conjured up an image of his wife gritting her teeth and clamping her legs together so the baby wouldn't pop out before he arrived. Surprised Shoshones glanced at him as he passed, but he ignored them. All he could think of was reaching his wife's side.

He half expected to find a small crowd gathered in front of Spotted Bull's lodge, or at the very least a few of the village women, but there was no one. It must be because most of the Shoshones had gone to see about Tall Grass's daughter, he reasoned, and covered the final 20 yards with the speed of a bounding antelope. The flap was open so he didn't bother with the social amenity of announcing his presence. He simply barged inside, then halted in astonishment.

Winona and Morning Dove were seated on the left side of the lodge, chatting. Neither appeared in the least bit agitated about the impending birth. They casually glanced up as he entered, and Winona smiled.

"I am glad you are here," she said.

Nate darted to her side. "Willow Woman told me you're about to have the baby."

"True," Winona said calmly.

"You can't be," Nate said, thinking that perhaps they had played a joke on him.

Winona's brow knit and she regarded him curiously. "I think I would know better than you."

"But why are you just sitting here? Where are the midwives? Shouldn't you be lying down? Shouldn't Morning Dove be boiling water?" Nate asked.

"Oh," Winona said in English and smiled. Then she changed to her own tongue again. "I have no need of a midwife. Morning Dove will prepare water for my cleansing while I am away. And I am sitting here waiting for you because walking would only hasten the birth."

Nate leaned over and studied her belly. "Are you certain now is the time?"

"Yes. The pains are very close now."

"Pains?" Nate said, aghast.

"Women experience regular pains before childbirth," Winona patiently explained. "Contractions deep inside."

"How soon will the baby be born?"

"As soon as you take me into the forest," Winona said and held up her right hand. "Please help me up."

"The forest?" Nate said. "Why can't you have it right here so Morning Dove can assist if necessary?"

"That is not our way. I am a grown woman and will drop the baby myself."

"But—" Nate began to protest, petrified at the idea of what might happen should he take her into the woods alone and a problem should arise.

"I have no time to discuss this," Winona said. "The pains are very close." She wagged her right hand. "Please help me up."

Swallowing hard, Nate dutifully complied, first leaning the Hawken against the lodge wall and then carefully lifting her to her feet. She immediately walked toward the entrance.

"Wait a minute," Nate said. "Shouldn't we take a medicine bag along or some blankets or a water bag or something?"

Winona sighed and stepped to a large buffalo robe that had been folded neatly and placed near the entrance. "This is all I will need. Please bring it."

"But—" Nate said, then hastened to the robe when she turned and walked out without waiting for him to finish. He started to follow, realized he had forgotten the Hawken, and dashed back to retrieve it. Morning Dove was looking at him as if he might be touched in the head. He grinned to show her he had everything under control, then whirled and ran outside, nearly colliding with Willow Woman, who had chosen that moment to return. "Sorry," he said and took off after his wife.

Winona was already ten yards to the east.

"Not so fast," Nate admonished her in English. "My guns aren't loaded. What if we run into a grizzly?"

"You can load them later," Winona said and walked

faster. Her mouth compressed into a thin line.

"Are you all right?" Nate asked anxiously, sticking close to her left side.

"As well as can be expected," Winona assured him in a strained tone. She abruptly grabbed hold of his arm for support. "I hope I have not waited too long, but I knew how much you wanted to be with me."

"I appreciate it," Nate said, almost wishing she had given birth while he was off fighting the mountain lion. His pulse raced, his mind whirled, and he couldn't seem to concentrate. He had never felt so nervous in all his born days. Whoever claimed having a child was easy had never known the torture a prospective father went through.

Winona picked up the pace, making a beeline through the lodges until they were out of the village. Then she headed for dense woodland.

Nate suspiciously scanned the wall of vegetation, dreading there might be hostile Indians out there, or maybe the mate of the panther he'd slain, or who knew what.

"We must find a sapling," Winona said.

"Why?" Nate asked, his attention focused on a bush that was shaking slightly. He gripped the hilt of his knife, then relaxed when a sparrow flew out of the bush.

"You will see," Winona told him. She placed both hands on her abdomen and grimaced. "We must hurry, husband, or I will have the baby right here."

Oh, Lord! Nate thought, and looked right and left as they entered the forest, seeking the type of tree she needed. But all the trees he saw were much older with thick trunks.

"Oh, my," Winona said softly. "Our baby is eager to enter this world."

Wait! Nate wanted to shout. For the love of God, please wait! He spied a sapling off to the left approximately 30 yards and steered Winona toward it. "There's one," he said. "Hang on. We're almost there."

"My legs are drenched," she said.

"Drenched? What do you mean by drenched?" Nate asked, fearing that she had accidentally urinated and the baby would be soiled.

"I will explain later," Winona said.

His heart pounding, Nate got her to the tree. She promptly gripped it with both hands, then glanced at him.

"Are you certain you want to see this?"

"Of course. I'm your husband. My place is right here with you," Nate assured her, although deep down he was terror-stricken. He recalled viewing the birth of a colt when he was eight or nine; he had nearly fainted from the sight. If he passed out on Winona, he'd never be able to hold his head high again.

"Please give me the robe."

"Here," Nate said, handing it to her. "Is there anything else I can do?"

"Not at the moment," Winona said, letting go of the sapling. She took the robe and spread it on the ground at the base of the tree, and as she unfolded it a small knife that had been wrapped inside rolled out.

"What's the knife for?" Nate inquired.

"You will see," Winona said, picking up the weapon and placing it at the edge of the robe. Then she raised her dress, pulling it above her waist, exposing her sleek thighs and her expanded belly.

Embarrassment assailed Nate. He glanced around, fearful of someone spotting them and beholding his wife's private parts. All he saw was a small finch flitting about in the trees, which reminded him that larger animals might well be prowling in the area. "I'm going to load my guns," he said.

Winona said nothing. She squatted and seized hold of the tree again, her knees outspread, her features etched in intense concentration, her bottom positioned over the soft robe.

Nate yanked the ramrod out of the Hawken, glad for the diversion. It gave him an excuse to take his mind and his eyes off the matter at hand. Working methodically, he measured out the proper amount of powder, fed it down the barrel, then wrapped a ball in a patch and rammed both into the rifle. Unable to take his eyes off Winona for very long, every 15 or 20 seconds he would glance at her. She continued to squat there, her chin bowed, her cheeks flushed. After a bit she commenced breathing loudly and regularly.

Why was she doing that? Nate wondered. He leaned the rifle against a nearby tree so he could load both flintlocks. The snap of a twig to his rear brought him around in alarm, but the cause turned out to be a chipmunk that took one look at him and fled as if a demon was on its heels. He swiftly finished with the two pistols and wedged them under his belt.

Winona gasped.

Nate faced her and saw her legs trembling, her bosom heaving as she began breathing even harder. Fascinated, he moved closer to be there if she needed him but she paid no attention. He wished he had asked more questions about the birth process. How long would it take? Did babies start crawling right away or did it take an hour or so for them to coordinate the movement of their limbs, as it did with certain farm animals? There was so much he didn't know and he regretted his ignorance.

Winona hunkered lower, her breaths loud enough now to be heard for yards. Her face was red and sweat beaded her brow.

"Anything I can do yet?" Nate asked on the off chance there might be. To his surprise, she ignored him. Feeling like a bump on a log, he surveyed the woods once more. Now there were three finches in a tree a few yards to the north. They were sitting quietly, staring at Winona as if equally fascinated by what was going on.

The breeze became stronger, stirring the leaves.

Nate rested his hands on the pistols and stepped nearer to Winona. He saw the muscles on her arms and legs quivering, saw her abdomen tightening, and realized she was straining with all of her might. The robe under her legs was wet, and a tangy scent unlike any he'd ever smelled tingled in his nostrils. To his great concern, Winona's breathing became even deeper.

A minute passed.

Two.

Five.

"Would you like some water?" Nate asked, anxious to do something. He began to doubt the wisdom of being by her side. What could he possibly accomplish that she couldn't? Maybe Lame Elk had been right. Giving birth should be a strictly feminine affair.

Again Winona made no comment, although she did look up for a few seconds and revealed her taut face and neck. Then she tucked her chin low and breathed with a rhythmic cadence.

Nate shifted uneasily, bothered by her silence. Was she mad at him, or was it simply hard for her to speak when she was focusing her entire energy on the birth? He gazed at her legs, then stiffened when he spied a dark object suspended from between them.

The baby!

He took a half-step and dropped to one knee. Sure enough, the top of a tiny head had poked out of the womb. The head was crowned with slick black hair, and the infant's face was as red as his Mackinaw coat. He couldn't determine if the baby's eyes were open yet or not, so he simply waved and beamed.

Suddenly voices sounded, coming from the direction of the village.

Spinning, Nate scanned the forest. He recognized the voices as female, and before long he spied three Shoshone women walking eastward, small baskets in their arms. Probably going to find herbs or roots, he guessed; by his estimation, the trio would pass within 15 feet of Winona. He stood and moved to intercept them.

One of the women spotted him and whispered to her companions. All three halted.

"Hello," Nate said, smiling to show he was friendly. He nodded at Winona. "My wife is having a baby. We need our privacy for the time being. Would you mind going well around us?"

The three Shoshones gazed past him, then talked excitedly. Finally, the shortest woman spoke. "Is your wife having a problem?"

"No. She is fine so far."

"Why are you here?"

"To do whatever I can," Nate said and became annoyed when they grinned and resumed whispering. "We really need to be by ourselves," he said and was grateful when they angled to the southeast and melted into the vegetation. They were bound to relate the encounter to their friends and relatives, and before long it would be common knowledge in the village. He might become the laughingstock of the tribe. But who cared? he asked himself. Winona was more important than idle gossip.

He heard Winona begin breathing in a nosier fashion, like a horse that had run five miles nonstop, and turned back in time to see the baby's head appear. Entranced, he edged closer. That was when he registered movement at the periphery of his vision and glanced to the north to discover the coyote.

Chapter Twelve

Nate jerked both flintlocks out and trained them on the slinking beast. He knew that coyotes sometimes hung around the outskirts of Indian villages in the hope of obtaining food. They would eat practically anything, and when butchered animal carcasses were tossed into the weeds, as often happened, the coyotes were there to gulp down whatever remained. And when the lodges were struck and a village moved on, coyotes frequently checked the campsite for edible scraps left behind or deliberately dumped.

This one happened to be a large male. It was wending through the undergrowth, fixedly gazing at Winona. Fifteen yards off the coyote halted.

Nate had never heard of coyotes attacking people and he was at a loss to explain the beast's behavior. With Winona preoccupied and unable to protect herself, he didn't want the coyote anywhere in the area. Wagging the pistols, he dashed toward it in an attempt to scare it off, not harm it.

The coyote held its ground for all of two seconds, then wheeled and sped off, its bushy tail held level with its body.

Stopping, Nate waited until the beast was gone before sticking the flintlocks under his brown belt and returning to his wife. Her entire body trembled from her supreme exertion. He moved to the left a bit for a better view of the baby and squatted.

The infant's head, neck, and a trace of its shoulders were out of Winona's womb, suspended just above the soft buffalo robe which was drenched by her fluids. The baby's eyes were closed, and it breathed shallowly.

Nate studied his offspring intently, mesmerized. He hadn't realized how small the child would be. Everything about it was tiny: tiny nose, tiny mouth, tiny ears, tiny hands, tiny fingers. It seemed so fragile that he was amazed it could survive the ordeal. His heart went out to the little treasure and joy filled him. Soon, if nothing went wrong, he would be a proud father, and he couldn't wait to hold the baby in his arms.

Was it a boy or a girl? He leaned forward, unable to determine the sex from the countenance or the small amount of hair. Winona was grunting, her eyes shut tight, oblivious to the world around her. He wanted to touch her, to let her know he was right there, but he was afraid the innocent gesture might break her concentration. A slight squishing noise drew his eyes to the baby, who had emerged a hair farther. The shoulders appeared to be wedged fast.

Winona began panting and rested her forehead on her forearm. Sweat coated her face and dripped from her legs. She spoke, the words almost inaudible, getting a word or two out between each pant. "Are you still here, husband?"

"No, I went to the lodge. Lame Elk and I are sitting around talking about the good old days," Nate said, grinning. "Need you ask?"

"Thank you."

"For what?"

"For you."

"I don't understand. What did I do?"

"How is the baby?"

"Fine, as near as I can tell," Nate said.

Nate glanced at the quietly resting infant. He wondered if Winona was aware that most of the baby was still up inside her. "Uh, dearest, there's something you should know."

"What?"

"The baby isn't all the way out yet."

"I know."

"You do? Then why have you stopped?" Nate asked. He blinked in bewilderment when she lifted her head and gave him a look capable of withering a plant at ten paces.

Winona sighed, adjusted her grip on the sapling, and strained.

Cocking his head, Nate watched the rest of the birth. Her thighs quivered and more fluid came out as the baby's shoulders slowly eased nearly all the way from her womb. She halted again, inhaling and gathering her strength, and when next she applied herself she wheezed mightily. He heard a plop as the shoulders finally slipped free, and he saw the infant slide onto the robe on its back.

It was a boy!

The word rang in Nate's head like the clanging of the church bell on a bright Sunday morning back in New York City. He almost laughed aloud in delight at the sight of the baby. In every respect the child was an exquisite copy of himself, although he noted definite traces of Winona's ancestry in the boy's face. He was amazed at how fragile and vulnerable newborn infants were, even more so than the colt he'd seen being born, and he pondered how dependent the child would be on Winona and him during his first few years of life.

What was that? Nate wondered when, to his surprise, he noticed a rope-like cord extending from the baby's stomach up into Winona. Then he realized it was the umbilical cord. Fortunately, the cord wasn't wrapped around the infant's neck, as occasionally happened. If it had been, his child might have emerged from the womb dead or been strangled during birth. Nate shuddered at the thought.

He emerged from his revery and realized that Winona wasn't done.

He listened to her grunt as she worked her stomach and leg muscles anew. The umbilical cord inched a bit lower, then stopped descending. Her whole body shook, yet still the cord hung in place. To him, it seemed as if it was taking her longer to drop the cord than the baby.

"Nate?"

"It's a boy," he told her proudly.

"A boy?" Winona asked. "The Great Medicine has been kind to us. The next time, though, I want a girl." She suddenly groaned.

Nate glanced up, saw his wife looking at him, and was shocked at the utter exhaustion he read in her drooping eyes and the deep lines in her face. "Yes?"

"I need your help."

"You do?" Nate said, confounded by the request. What in the world could he do to assist at this stage of the birth? A disturbing possibility occurred to him and his gaze dropped to between her legs.

"Pull it out."

"Me?"

"It is stuck."

"Me?"

"Is our son sitting up yet?"

"No."

"Then it must be you," Winona said wearily. "I am

tired, Nate. So tired. Please. We can go back once it is done and I can rest."

"I'd rather not."

"Is the great Grizzly Killer afraid?"

"Scared to death," Nate said and reluctantly bent forward, his hair brushing her leg as he tentatively reached under her to gently grasp the spongy umbilical cord. Her sweet scent engulfed him. Queasiness flooded through him and he clamped his mouth shut to prevent the contents of his stomach from mixing with the puddle of blood and other fluid already soaking into the robe. The touch of the cord brought gooseflesh to every square inch of his skin.

"Pull slowly," Winona cautioned. "Do not break it."

"Lord, help me," Nate said, and did as she wanted, terrified of making a mistake and snapping the cord in half. If the afterbirth didn't come out, she might sicken and die. It had happened to other women, which was why doctors took such careful pains to guarantee every last bit was removed.

"Slowly," Winona said again.

As if pulling on the delicate stem of a flower, Nate gently applied enough force to draw the cord slowly lower. Inch by gradual inch, it came out. Suddenly the cord stopped. Deep inside her the afterbirth had encountered an obstruction or was somehow snagged. He tugged lightly, but the cord wouldn't budge.

"What has happened?" Winona asked.

"I don't rightly know," Nate said, feeling sweat form under his arms. "It's stuck again. Maybe I should run to the village and get Morning Dove or Willow Woman."

"And leave our son and me here alone?"

Nate frowned at his stupidity. "No, I guess not."

"Keep trying. I trust you."

"Thanks," Nate said, wishing he trusted his own ability half as much as she did. He lay on his stomach and reached higher, grasping the cord just below her body, his fingers brushing against her as he pulled once more. The added leverage helped. Abruptly, the umbilical cord eased out and brought with it the rest of the afterbirth, falling clear of her body onto his right hand. He brought his arm out from under her and stared in horrified astonishment at the eerie mass clinging to his flesh. For a few moments he felt dizzy and worried he might humiliate himself by fainting.

"It's out, isn't it?" Winona asked.

Nate went to answer but his mouth was completely dry. The best he could do was imitate a tree frog.

"What?" Winona said. "Can you see the afterbirth? Is it out?"

"It's out," Nate managed to say.

"Are you all right?"

"Never better," Nate fibbed and placed the afterbirth on the robe. He rose, his knees unsteady, and mechanically brushed dirt and bits of grass from his buckskins.

Winona, her features contorted, painfully straightened until her knees audibly popped. As she moved haltingly to one side, her dress fell down around her ankles. She gazed down at the baby, happiness replacing her discomfort. "Our son," she said with pride.

"Want me to carry him back?" Nate said.

"There is something I must do first," Winona said and sank to her knees beside the baby. She caressed its cheeks and head, cooing tenderly in Shoshone, then traced a finger around the umbilical cord where it was attached to the child's abdomen.

Mystified, Nate watched her examine the cord. All was explained the instant she picked up the small knife she had brought along. "Are you fixing to cut the cord?" he asked.

"Unless you would rather do it?"

"Go ahead," Nate said and casually placed a hand

over his mouth to be on the safe side. The vertigo struck him again when she started to slice and he had to turn away to suppress another bout of sickness. His whole body shuddered. He didn't dare risk a peek as she finished her task. A minute went by.

"Here. You can hold him now."

Nate turned, relieved to see that she had swaddled their son in a clean corner of the buffalo robe. The rest of the robe dangled underneath. He took the bundle in his arms, amazed at how dainty the child was, and felt unbridled love course through his being for his wife and the new pride of their life. At that moment, in that time and place, in that heartbeat of eternity, his love was pure and absolute, bordering on reverence. Was this how every new father felt?

Using the tree for support, Winona stood. "We must hurry," she said. "He must be bathed and wrapped in a clean blanket before he becomes sick."

"Lean on me," Nate told her. She put her left hand on his shoulder and took a step that any self-respecting snail could have beaten. "You were magnificent," he complimented her, staying by her side as she walked westward.

Winona beamed. "So were you. I am glad you insisted on being there. If you had not been, I would never have gotten the afterbirth out."

"You'll be fine once you've rested," Nate said and twisted his head to peck her on the cheek. "I've never seen anyone work so hard at anything. You must want to sleep around the clock."

"No, although you would think that would be the case," Winona said. "My strength is returning quickly. By tomorrow I will be up and about as if nothing had happened."

"Don't push yourself," Nate cautioned and glanced at the baby. Something about the child was different, and it wasn't until the infant blinked that he realized his son's eyes were open. "Look," he exclaimed. "His eyes are brown."

Winona stared affectionately at their offspring and rested her head on Nate's broad shoulder. "We must select a name for him."

"So soon?"

"It is the custom of my people to pick a name before a sleep has gone by," Winona said, then tilted her head upward. "I did not think to ask. Do you want to give him a Shoshone name or a white man's name?"

"Why not both?"

"A fine idea," Winona said. "Then he will be at home in both worlds." She straightened and surveyed the forest around them, a shadow creeping over her face. "I see nothing worth naming a son after, not even an animal."

"Too bad you weren't paying attention while you were giving birth," Nate said. "A coyote tried to sneak up on you but I chased the critter off."

"A coyote?"

"Yep. One of the biggest male coyotes I've ever laid eyes on," Nate confirmed.

"It is an omen."

"What?"

Winona laughed and squeezed his arm in her gaiety. "A sign from the Everywhere Spirit. Don't you see, husband? We are supposed to name our son Sneaking Coyote."

Nate snorted. "Like hell we will."

"I beg your pardon?"

"No son of mine is going around with a name that implies he skulks about like a thief in the night," Nate said. "I don't mind the Coyote part, but the first half has to go." He pondered for a minute. "How about Stalking Coyote? It has a ring to it, just like a warrior's name should."

"Stalking Coyote," Winona repeated, rolling the

words on her tongue. "Yes, I like it very much. But what about his other name?"

"It goes without saying that his last name will be King," Nate noted. "As for his first name, there is one I've been partial to ever since I was a boy."

"What is it?"

"Orville."

Winona scrunched up her nose as if she'd inhaled a bitter odor. "Orville?"

"Yes. What's wrong with it?"

"It is difficult to describe. The best I can do is say it offends my ears. Perhaps you should pick another name."

"I've always liked Orville."

"Please. I agreed to change when you were upset."

"True," Nate said, racking his brain for another name worthy of being bestowed on their son. Finally the perfect choice occurred to him. "I have another suggestion. It was the name of my great-great-grandfather, and I like it almost as much as I do Orville."

"What is this one?" Winona asked uncertainly.

"Zachary."

"I like it," Winona said without hesitation. "Zachary King is a fine name."

"Then we're agreed," Nate said and lifted their child higher so he could lightly kiss the boy on the forehead. "Zachary King and Stalking Coyote it is. Now let's go introduce you to your mother's people."

"Yours also, husband."

Chapter Thirteen

The next three days were some of the happiest of Nate's entire life. He basked in the profound happiness of having a new son, and took great comfort in the steady string of well-wishers who stopped by Spotted Bull's lodge to relay their congratulations and kind regards. The Shoshones revered all life, as did most Indian tribes, and they took particular delight in newborns. They saw spirit omens in everything, and infants, especially male infants, were regarded as confirmation of the Everywhere Spirit's blessing.

The birth of Stalking Coyote, following as it did so closely on the heels of the incident with the mountain lion, convinced the Shoshones that Nate was a man who brought good fortune on himself and others. Several prominent warriors told him outright that he possessed great medicine, and he basked in their esteem and good will.

To make matters complete, Nate was elated when the council decided to let Red Hawk stay at the village for as long as he wanted. The leaders of the tribe had decided that any man willing to risk his life to save a Shoshone child was a true friend of their people. Spotted Bull insisted on permitting Red Hawk to stay with him.

So on the fourth day Nate sat outside of the lodge, feeling the warmth of the morning sun on his face, and counted himself fortunate at the way things had worked out. He had a new son, a new friend, and a new appreciation of the Shoshones. After their marvelous display of friendship, he felt more at home among them than he ever had before. He heard footsteps, and around the corner came his host and the Oglala. "How do you like your new horses?" he inquired using sign.

"They are fine animals," Red Hawk replied in kind and looked at Spotted Bull. "I appreciate your generosity, but I will never be able to give you a gift of equal value."

"A gift should never be given with thought of a reward," Spotted Bull said. "And you will need horses if you hope to have your own lodge."

"What is this?" Nate asked.

Red Hawk took a seat. "I cannot stay in Spotted Bull's lodge forever. It would be unfair to his family." He gazed out over the lake. "I have been giving the matter much thought, and I have decided to live among the Shoshones until my breath fades away on the wind. They have accepted me without question. They have given me the chance to start my life over. To do that, I need my own lodge. Only then can I hope to acquire a wife."

"A lodge will be easy to make once you have enough buffalo hides and poles," Nate said.

"A man can get poles any time," Red Hawk signed. "Buffalo hides take longer to collect. First enough buffalo must be slain, and hunting them down one or two at a time could take two moons or more."

"I know," Nate said. Buffalo tended to take flight at the first sight or scent of humans. Once a hunter loosed an arrow or fired a shot, the rest of any given herd would pound off into the distance as fast as their heavy legs would take them. So when a man needed to kill more than one, he had to take companions along and hope each was lucky; or he could spend weeks stalking any buffalo he spied, but this method was a tedious and not infrequently futile exercise. Because even if the hunt did score a hit, there was no guarantee the buffalo would fall. Buffalo were exceptionally hardy animals, almost as hard to kill as grizzlies. There had been verified instances where a buffalo bristling with a dozen arrows or pierced by five to ten balls had fled and eluded the hapless men after it.

Nate didn't envy Red Hawk his task. Slaying buffalo was only the first step in going about making a lodge. Depending on the projected size of the structure, a dozen or more large hides might be required and each one had to be meticulously skinned from the carcass, then diligently prepared to make it waterproof yet resilient.

"I know of a way you can obtain all the hides you might need at one time," Spotted Bull signed.

"How?" Red Hawk asked.

"Join us in a surround."

In all the excitement of the past few days, Nate had completely forgotten about the planned surround. The reminder jarred him. He felt certain that Spotted Bull would again ask him to go along, and this time he couldn't plead his son's birth as an excuse. He still didn't want to participate in the hunt. Unfortunately, since surrounds were considered tests of bravery and skill, any man who repeatedly refused to go on one stood the risk of having his manhood questioned. If he was to decline graciously again, he must have a legitimate excuse for not going. He listened attentively to their conversation.

"I have been on surrounds before," Red Hawk said. "They are grisly business. Many of your warriors might die."

"We are aware of the risks," Spotted Bull said. "The Oglalas are not the only people who know how to properly hunt buffalo."

"When are you leaving?" Red Hawk asked.

"In two or three sleeps."

Red Hawk reflected for a moment. "All right. I will go with you. Perhaps, if I am lucky, I will kill many buffalo and my lodge will be completed that much sooner."

"We will be glad to have you ride with us," Spotted Bull said. "And I would not worry much about the danger. So many good omens have taken place in the past few days that every warrior in our village is confident this will be the best surround we have ever taken part in."

"I pray you are right," Red Hawk said.

Spotted Bull glanced at Nate. "The hunt would go all that much better if the man many believe carries good fortune on his shoulders would come with us."

An icy finger stabbed into Nate's chest. He knew the Shoshone was referring to him, and he deliberately stared at a snowcapped mountain situated north of the encampment to give the false impression that he wasn't paying attention.

"Grizzly Killer?" Spotted Bull said aloud.

Nate's heart sank. He couldn't avoid the inevitable. "Yes?" he answered, facing his host.

"Now that your son has been born, would you agree to accompany myself and the other warriors who are going on the surround? We would be very honored," Spotted Bull signed.

Nate suppressed an automatic impulse to frown. There was no way out. If he declined, by nightfall every man in the tribe would know. He would be the main topic of discussion around every lodge fire, with everyone in the village speculating on the reason for his refusal. They might doubt his bravery, or they might mistakenly believe that he knew something they didn't, that he had experienced a dire premonition and expected the hunting party to meet with disaster. They would take the refusal as a bad omen. His future relations with the tribe could be severely jeopardized by his answer, and he disliked being put on the spot. He tried not to let his resentment show as he replied, "I would be delighted to go with you."

Spotted Bull grinned. "This is great news. Excuse me while I go inform the others who are going." He headed off at a brisk clip, saying over his shoulder, "I would not be surprised if more warriors decided to go once they learn you will be along."

Nate plastered a phony smile on his face until the Shoshone was out of sight. He glanced at Red Hawk and found the Oglala studying him critically. "You have something to say?" Nate signed.

"If you do not want to go, why not tell Spotted Bull the truth?"

"Is it that obvious?" Nate asked.

"To me," Red Hawk signed. "Even though I have not known you long, I feel as if I know you as well as I do my own brother."

"You have a brother?"

"Two. Both married with children."

"Do you miss them?"

"Of course," Red Hawk signed. "We were always in each other's company. In our childhood we played, rode horses, and practiced with weapons together. When we became grown men we hunted, went on raids, and even took our brides at the same time so we could be married together." He smiled wistfully. "I miss them most of all."

"Maybe one day you will see them again," Nate said.

"If I do, they would be forced to slay me. An outcast who tries to return is always put to death. They could not spare me because we are related."

Nate felt a burning curiosity to inquire about the specific details behind his friend's expulsion, but he wisely refrained. "I am glad things have worked out for you here," he said. "You have a new home. The Shoshones accept you as one of their own, so your wandering days are over."

"And I owe it all to you," Red Hawk signed.

From inside the lodge arose light feminine laughter. Nate glanced at the closed flap and mulled over how best to inform Winona of his upcoming departure. The direct approach would only upset her. He had to exercise tact.

Red Hawk stood. "I am going to take another walk around the village," he signed. "After being alone for so long, I find that I like to mingle with people more than I ever did." He surveyed the village, his eyes alight with contentment. "These are my people now, and I must get to know them like I know my own."

"Enjoy yourself," Nate said and watched the warrior stroll away. He shoved to his feet, stepped to the lodge, and slapped the flap. "It's me," he called out in English. "Are all of you decent?"

"What a silly question," Winona said. "Shoshone women are not like the Otos. We do not sit around naked in our lodges. Come in, husband."

Nate entered. His wife sat to the left, cradling little Zachary King in her arms. The baby had been bundled in a blanket, leaving only the top of his head visible. Morning Dove was busy at the cooking pot, while

Willow Woman was sorting through a parflache in the far corner. He walked over and sat down next to Winona. "How is our son?"

"Sleeping soundly," Winona said and parted the blanket to reveal Zachary's tranquil features. She tenderly stroked the infant's rounded chin. "Would you care to hold him?"

"He looks comfortable right where he is," Nate said, glad they could speak English and not be understood by the other women. "I don't want to wake him up." He leaned closer, proudly examining their son's face, and said softly, "Stalking Coyote is in perfect health, isn't he?"

"Yes," Winona said. "We have been blessed with a fine son. He hasn't cried once yet."

"When they're this age," Nate said, "taking care of them is easy. One parent can do it with no problem."

Winona regarded him thoughtfully for a full 15 seconds before she asked, "What are you getting at?"

"I have something to tell you," Nate said, refusing to meet her probing gaze. He should have known she would realize he was beating around the bush. Now he must come right out with it. The thought of deserting her so soon after their son had been born racked him with guilt. At least, he rationalized, she would be among relatives and friends, so it wasn't the same as when he occasionally left her alone at their cabin to go off trapping or whatever.

Winona waited expectantly.

"Spotted Bull asked me to go on the surround," Nate said.

"What did you tell him?"

"What could I tell him?" Nate asked, finally looking at her. "I told him I would go."

Anxiety lined Winona's countenance. "I do not like it," she said flatly. "You have never been on a surround before. It's not fair that they should want you to go when our son was born just a few days ago."

"I agree, but there's nothing I can do."

Winona placed a hand on his shoulder. "You can let him know you have changed your mind. Wait until tomorrow and tell him you had a bad dream while you slept. Tell him that you saw yourself being gored. He will understand."

"I would be lying," Nate said. "And I have already given my word. There is no way out. When the warriors leave on the great hunt, I'll be with them."

"And if something happens to you? What will I do then?"

"Take good care of our son," Nate said and felt her fingers dig into him. He placed a hand on hers and patted it. "Don't worry. I'm not about to make you a widow after all the trouble you went through."

"No man can predict his time," Winona said.

"You sure know how to cheer a man up," Nate said, trying to make light of the situation, hoping to bring a smile to her lips. Instead, she scowled.

"I am not trying to cheer you up. I am trying to convince you that you are taking your life in your hands if you go," Winona said earnestly. "I lost a cousin and two close friends to surrounds when I was a girl, and I have never forgotten the way their bodies looked after the buffalo were done with them."

"I can imagine," Nate said. He touched her cheek and kissed her. "Mark my words, dearest. If it's humanly possible, I will return."

Refusing to be comforted, Winona held their son to her bosom and said sadly, "Words are no match for buffalo horns."

Chapter Fourteen

Two days later 41 riders rode eastward from Clear Lake. Forty were in exuberant spirits, talking and laughing and singing, while one rode in somber silence at the head of the band wishing he was somewhere else. Most of the villagers turned out for the departure, with the women waving and smiling and the children dashing playfully around the mounted men.

Nate would never forget the haunted aspect to Winona's eyes as she bid him farewell. He got the impression she never expected to see him again, although she had never come right out and said so. For the better part of 48 hours she had moped around the lodge, her usual cheerful disposition replaced by moody preoccupation with the surround.

And she hadn't been the only one.

Nate had noticed both Morning Dove and Willow Woman become unusually taciturn the closer it grew to the appointed time for leaving. Morning Dove's attitude he could comprehend; she was concerned about Spotted Bull. But Willow Woman's melancholy had puzzled him at first. He'd attributed her feelings to her affection for her father, although at times she seemed even more upset than her mother. Then he'd seen Willow Woman and Red Hawk strolling along the lake, their shoulders occasionally brushing together as they chatted amiably, the one always glancing at the other when the other wasn't looking, and he could have slapped himself for being such a dunderhead.

Afterwards, he noticed other things. Such as how Willow Woman had taken to doting over Red Hawk, giving him extra portions at meal times and preparing his bedding at night. She was even sewing a pair of leggings for him. And once, when Nate unexpectedly entered the lodge, he caught them kissing. No one else had been there at the time, and he had quickly backed out.

The only one Nate told about his discovery was Winona, and she had actually grinned and asked why it had taken so long for him to see the obvious. Apparently everyone else in the lodge knew of the budding romance, which had Spotted Bull's blessing. The Shoshone had taken Red Hawk under his wing and regarded him as a second son.

The first son, Touch The Clouds, showed up at the lodge the day before the 40 warriors were to leave for the surround. He had been off hunting elk with friends and consequently learned of the encounter with the mountain lion after his return. He'd immediately gone to his father's lodge to pay his respects to the famous Grizzly Killer and the Oglala.

Of all the men Nate had ever met, Touch The Clouds was the biggest. A veritable giant, standing close to seven feet tall and endowed with a powerful physique, Touch The Clouds appeared capable of fighting a grizzly with his bare hands and emerging triumphant.

When he entered a lodge he had to squeeze through the entrance, and if he was to straighten too quickly, he often bumped his head. When he rode his warhorse, it was as if he rode a pony even though his splendid black stallion was larger than any other horse in the camp. His war club was three times the size of those carried by his fellow warriors, and his bow could shoot twice as far. His lance resembled a lodge pole. All in all, it was no wonder that Touch The Clouds was widely regarded as the single bravest warrior in the Shoshone nation although he had yet to count as many coup as some of the older men.

Now Nate rode between the giant on his left and Spotted Bull on his right. Behind them came Red Hawk, White Lynx, and Drags The Rope. The rest of the hunters were clustered in groups and strung out over 50 yards to the rear.

"Where should we seek the herds, father?" Touch The Clouds asked.

Spotted Bull, as befitted his status as the leader of the hunters, was responsible for making the major decisions pertaining to their course of travel and the sites they would select as their nightly camps. He scratched his chin, his brow knit in thought. "I told Broken Paw that we would head toward the Greasy Grass River country. Buffalo are always plentiful there at this time of the year."

"So are the Arapaho, Cheyenne, and Crow," Touch The Clouds said.

"We will stay to the west of their usual hunting grounds," Spotted Bull said. "If the Everywhere Spirit smiles on us, we will not run into them. And once the rest of our people have established a village in the foothills, there will be so many of us that the Arapahos, Cheyennes, and Crows dare not attack."

Nate tensed and glanced at him. "What is this about the rest of your people?"

"Surely someone told you," Spotted Bull said. "Those we left behind will strike camp tomorrow morning, and within six or seven sleeps they will have set up a new village near the area where we will be hunting."

"Everyone will come there?"

"Of course."

Flabbergasted, Nate stared straight ahead. No one had bothered to mention the entire village would move to be closer to the surround. Winona had not said a word, either because she'd believed he would object to her being in close proximity to hostile territory or because, like the rest of her tribe, she had taken it for granted that he would know the whole tribe would relocate.

"Why are you so surprised?" Spotted Bull asked.

"No one bothered to tell me," Nate said lamely.

"Who do you think will butcher the buffalo we slay?" Touch The Clouds said. "Warriors don't do the work of women. By moving the village to the foothills, the women will be near at hand when the surround is over and can skin the animals on the spot."

"We go ahead of the main camp because such a large number of people often scares the buffalo away," Spotted Bull said. "We will find a herd the proper size and keep watch over it until the village is in place. If the buffalo wander, we will keep track of where they go." He paused. "A surround must be well thought out or it will fail."

"So I see," Nate said. He made a mental note to have a long talk with Winona once they were reunited.

"I hope to take fifteen buffalo, at least," Touch The Clouds said. "I can use a new lodge."

"The one you have now is only two winters old," Spotted Bull said.

"And already it shows signs of wear and has been repaired in several spots," Touch The Clouds said.

Spotted Bull looked at Nate. "Perhaps Lame Elk was right," he said, his eyes twinkling.

Nate politely smiled, his mind not on their discussion. All he could think of was the fact that they were going to enter the hunting grounds traditionally used by the tribes who dwelled on the Plains, and how the Arapahos and others were bound to resent the intrusion. He wasn't as optimistic as Spotted Bull; if something could go wrong, it invariably did. Which meant the Shoshones might find themselves embroiled in tribal warfare with one of the powerful nations inhabiting the region adjacent to the Greasy Grass River. He didn't like the idea one bit.

"I will be content with one buffalo," Spotted Bull said. "I have it in my heart to give Morning Dove a new robe as a gift, and the wife of a friend has agreed to make it if I supply the hide." He grinned. "Morning Dove will be very surprised."

"You're going on a surround for just one robe?" Nate asked in disbelief.

"It is part of my plan."

"I do not understand."

"If I were to go off hunting buffalo by myself, Morning Dove might guess that I intend to give her a new robe," Spotted Bull said. "This way, she will have no idea. It would never occur to her that I would go on a surround just to obtain a single hide."

"Nor anyone else," Nate said dryly.

"I am proud of you, father," Touch The Clouds said. "It is a kind gesture. I hope my wife and I are still as much in love when we are your age."

"Never take your wife for granted," Spotted Bull said, "never let her take you for granted, and your marriage will last until you are both gray-haired and ready to depart this world."

Nate absently bobbed his chin in agreement. He'd never discussed marriage with a warrior before and found the insights fascinating. "I agree with you. But there are other factors that go into making a successful marriage."

"True," Spotted Bull said. "Loyalty, a calm tongue, and a sense of humor."

"A sense of humor?"

"People who cannot laugh at their own mistakes take themselves far too seriously to be able to get along well with others. Life was meant for laughing."

"Never thought of it that way."

"I think loyalty is the most important," Touch The Clouds said. "Without loyalty, a couple will quickly drift apart. If the man's eyes stray to other women and the wife's to other men, they might as well not get married."

"Their eyes would not stray if they would remember that the true beauty of a person is not found on the outside, but deep inside. When I was a young married man and I found myself looking at another pretty woman, thinking of how nice it would be to lie with her under my robe, I always reminded myself that I already had a woman who kept me warm at night and she did not mind touching my cold feet."

Nate laughed heartily. For the next several hours he conversed with the Shoshones about everything from proper hunting techniques to ways to determine changes in the weather. At midday Spotted Bull called a halt on the bank of a stream and the warriors watered their mounts. Drags The Rope walked up to Nate as he was checking the cinch on his saddle.

"This will be a fine hunt, my friend. I had a dream last night that I killed nine buffalo."

"I am eager to find the herd," Nate said, neglecting to mention that he was also eager to get the surround over with so he could spend time with Winona and Zachary.

"If I do well, it will greatly impress Singing Bird,"

Drags The Rope said. "She will gladly give her word to marry me." He paused. "I have wanted to ask you about Shakespeare. I thought the two of you were inseparable. Where is he?"

"He went and got himself married to a Flathead woman. I haven't seen him in a while, but when this is over I intend to swing by his cabin and see if he's back home yet."

Drags The Rope smirked. "Shakespeare too. I guess the saying is true."

"What saying?"

"A warrior is never too old to be stung by a bee while collecting honey."

Soon they were back on their horses and heading ever eastward, wending among stark, towering peaks that seemed to touch the pillowy white clouds floating far overhead. They traversed lush valleys, crossed grassy meadows, and skirted high ridges. The Rocky Mountain wildlife, as always, was abundant, and they spotted scores of deer and elk, as well as smaller game such as rabbits, squirrels, and chipmunks.

By the end of the first day Nate began to thoroughly enjoy himself. Or at least, he tried to. But every time he let himself get into the spirit of things, guilt at being away from his family would spoil his good mood. He kept thinking of Winona, who undoubtedly was miserable, pining for him back at the village, and he couldn't bring himself to be happy when he knew she wasn't. Then he would become involved in a lively discussion and forget all about her until he had a spare moment to reflect and realized his oversight, at which point he would be racked with guilt again.

Since he wasn't selected to pull sentry duty, Nate slept soundly the whole night through, exhausted more by his emotional turmoil than the many hours in the saddle. He was roused out of slumber the next morning by Drags The Rope, and together they shuffled to the stream to drink and splash frigid water on their faces. It was the part of traveling that Nate liked the least. There was something about being transformed into gooseflesh the first thing in the morning that smacked of outright torture.

After a breakfast of jerked venison and pemmican, the Shoshones resumed their journey. Nate noticed that the warriors were not quite as lighthearted as the day before. Indeed, the closer they drew to prime buffalo country, which also happened to be the hunting grounds of their many enemies, the more subdued the Shoshones became. By the afternoon of the second day, Spotted Bull had selected four men to ride half a mile ahead of the main group. He was taking no chances.

Nate got to know other warriors quite well. There was Little Beaver, who stood only an inch over five feet but could shoot an arrow with uncanny precision. There was Worm, who had lost his left ear and half of his face to a grizzly. And there was Lone Wolf, who had three wives and was considering taking another.

From his talks, Nate learned that about half of the Shoshone men had more than one wife. The shortage of warriors was the main reason; there simply weren't enough men to go around. Many of the men, though, such as Spotted Bull, disliked the idea of having two or three wives and steadfastly refused to do so. Which pleased Lone Wolf no end, because then there were more women to go around to those warriors who wanted them.

That afternoon, as they ascended a low hill, Lone Wolf turned to Nate in all earnestness and said, "You should take another wife or two for your own. You will be a happier man if you do."

"You think so?" Nate said, suppressing a grin.

"Most definitely," Lone Wolf said. "Think of the benefits. Your lodge will always be clean and kept in perfect condition. The women will compete with each other to see who can make you the best food. And at night, there will always be at least one who is in the mood for love." He grinned. "I could never go back to having one wife now that I know the joys of having three."

"You are a braver man than I am," Nate said.

"What do—" Lone Wolf began, then stopped speaking and reined up sharply.

Nate automatically did the same. He saw that Spotted Bull had halted and was peering intently to the northwest.

Not a quarter of a mile away was another large band of Indians.

Chapter Fifteen

All the Shoshones came to a stop.

Nate shielded his eyes from the bright sun with his left hand, trying to identify the other party. They were too far off for him to note much detail except that they were on foot. He hoped—he prayed—they weren't Blackfeet.

"Bloods," Touch The Clouds said.

"Twenty-four of them," Drags The Rope added.

The news caused Nate's pulse to quicken. The Bloods were allies of the Blackfeet, who enjoyed a fierce reputation in their own right. He'd tangled with them once before and barely escaped with his hide.

"They have seen us," Spotted Bull said.

The Bloods were aligned in the formation they typically used when a war party was on the march. They stood in a single file arranged in the shape of a crescent with the central arc out in front of the curved arms. They were crossing the open slope of a mountain; in another minute, they would have been into dense forest.

"Our scouts missed seeing them," Touch The Clouds said.

"They were probably not in sight when our scouts went over this hill," Spotted Bull said. He twisted to scan the rest of the Shoshones, his face alight with excitement. "This is an opportunity we cannot let pass. We outnumber them, and we have horses. They will not be able to run away. I say we attack them and take as many scalps as we can."

"Yes!" Touch The Clouds said, hefting his huge lance.

Nate looked at the others, hoping a voice of reason would be raised. But the warriors all vented whoops of joy at the prospect of bloody battle. Wildly waving their weapons in the air, they worked themselves into a fever pitch. He wondered whether he should object, reminding them that they were after buffalo hides, not scalps.

With a strident shriek, Spotted Bull urged his horse down the hill, leading the charge. The rest of the Shoshones fell in behind him, forming a screeching mass of bloodthirsty riders each anxious to claim the first coup.

Nate found himself left behind. He goaded the stallion into a run, trailing the rest by ten yards or more, firming his grip on the Hawken. The ground was rough, dotted with fallen trees and lined with shallow gullies. He had to concentrate exclusively on avoiding all obstacles and keeping the Shoshones in sight, and before he knew it they were almost to the mountain slope. He looked up to find that the Bloods had disappeared into the trees, where they would be able to give a good account of themselves, and he dreaded a slaughter if the Shoshones rode into a hail of arrows.

Spotted Bull apparently had the same thought. He

angled into the forest well below the spot where the Bloods had been and promptly slowed. The other warriors fanned out, forming a skirmish line, staying on their horses so they could see farther even though it made them better targets.

Nate caught up with them shortly after they spread out. He took up a position near Red Hawk, who had stayed with the Shoshones every step of the way. Before them lay thick undergrowth and tall trees. Underfoot lay a carpet of pine needles and matted vegetation. A deathly silence shrouded the wilderness.

Nate wondered if the Bloods would employ a tactic invariably resorted to by the Blackfeet when they were on the defensive. When pressed, the Blackfeet would hastily erect conical forts constructed from long tree limbs, then wage their fight from inside such crude shelters. The forts were proof against arrows and lances, but they were of little protection against guns. Once a group of trappers had surrounded a fort occupied by ten Blackfeet and slain all but one simply by shooting into the center of the structure.

Something moved up ahead.

Leaning low over the pommel to minimize his silhouette, Nate scoured the forest. Since the Bloods hadn't had the time to erect forts, they would try to spring an ambush at any moment, and Nate didn't intend to be on the receiving end of one of their barbed shafts.

Spotted Bull and Touch The Clouds had pulled slightly in front of the others. The giant held his lance poised to throw.

Suddenly harsh cries rent the stillness, and the Bloods swarmed from concealment in a frenzy of swirling tomahawks and war clubs. Several employed bows with lethal effect.

In the opening moments of the battle Nate saw three Shoshones go down, and then the band retaliated with vigor, bearing down on their enemies and fighting man to man, many leaping from their horses and forsaking their height advantage to get in close. He marveled that few of the Shoshones used their bows, but then recalled that it was considered far braver for a warrior to kill with a club or a tomahawk than to kill from a distance with an arrow. The highest coup always went to those who slew their foes in personal combat.

The next moment reflection became impossible. A beefy Blood dashed toward him, a war club uplifted to strike. Nate felt no compunction about killing from a distance; the Blood was still 12 feet away when he took a hasty bead and fired, his ball coring the man's brain and flipping the warrior onto his back.

He wrenched on the reins, bringing his stallion to a halt behind a pine tree, and grabbed his powder horn to reload. To his right was Red Hawk, still mounted and trying to pierce a Blood with his lance. The Blood pranced just out of range, waving a tomahawk and taunting the Oglala to try harder.

Nate spied another Blood, armed with a war club, closing on Red Hawk from the rear. He quickly drew his right flintlock, extended the pistol, and when the Blood drew back an arm to smash the war club against Red Hawk's spine, he fired. Lead and smoke spurted from the pistol at the sharp report, and a hole blossomed in the center of the Blood's chest. The warrior clutched at the wound, screamed, and pitched onto his face.

All around Nate was a whirling melee of savage combatants. The Bloods, for the most part, were naked from the waist up and had their faces painted for war. Otherwise, Nate would have had a difficult time telling the two factions apart.

He constantly glanced right and left, his body tingling in expectation of being hit by an arrow, as he hurriedly reloaded the flintlock, then the rifle. When under pressure he could load any of his weapons in under 30 seconds. This time he did the two in under forty.

The Shoshones were keeping the Bloods busy. Outnumbered, the Bloods fought valiantly, refusing to give up. Bodies dotted the ground, some twitching and convulsing. A horse was down on its side, accidentally struck in the neck by an arrow.

Nate tried to keep track of his friends, but the task was hopeless. He'd lost sight of Spotted Bull and Touch The Clouds. Drags The Rope was off somewhere to the west. Red Hawk had dispatched the prancing Blood and was now after another.

A strident chorus of whoops and yells filled the woods, mixed intermittently with the death wail of a dying warrior. Bedlam and unbridled brutality reigned throughout the forest.

Wedging the reloaded pistol under his belt, Nate rode forward, prepared to aid Shoshones in trouble, but not intending to become actively involved unless put upon. Almost immediately, he was. A lean Blood, a tomahawk in one hand and a bloody scalp in the other, bounded at him with the feline grace of a lynx about to spring on its prey.

Nate didn't have time to aim. He simply pointed the Hawken in the Blood's direction and hastily fired, the rifle recoiling as it boomed. The ball smash into the warrior's forehead. Then the Blood stumbled forward, propelled by his momentum, and thudded to the earth at the stallion's feet.

An arrow streaked out of nowhere and smacked into a nearby tree.

To the right a Shoshone and a Blood were grappling on the ground, locked in a grim clash to the death.

Nate kept going. If he stayed in one spot, he practically invited the Bloods to use him as a pincushion. He drew his pistol again and twisted this way and that, trying to see every which way at once. The short hairs at the nape of his neck prickled, but he resisted an urge to wheel his horse and race to safety.

The stallion abruptly shied, and Nate looked down to see a dead Shoshone in their path. Jerking on the reins, he skirted the corpse. From the sound of the conflict, it appeared the battle was drifting to the northwest. Perhaps the Bloods had finally realized they couldn't win and were retreating.

A rider appeared, coming slowly toward him, swaying on his animal, his arms limp at his sides.

Nate moved to help the man. He was almost to the warrior's side before he recognized Little Beaver and saw the feathered end of an arrow sticking out of the base of the Shoshone's throat. "Little Beaver!" he said and drew alongside the warrior just as his injured friend started to fall. With a rifle and the reins in one hand and a pistol in the other, there was little Nate could do other than throw out an arm in an attempt stop the Shoshone from toppling. He managed to brace his right forearm against the warrior's shoulder, checking the fall.

Little Beaver's eyes were closed. They suddenly fluttered and opened, and he looked at Nate. "Grizzly Killer?" he said softly. "I am so cold." As he spoke, blood spurted from the corners of his mouth.

"I will help you," Nate said and went to slip the pistol under his belt.

"Tell my wife I was thinking of her," Little Beaver said and keeled over backwards, a protracted breath fluttering from his lips.

"No!" Nate cried and tried to clutch the warrior's hand. He missed, and the next moment Little Beaver dropped to the pine needles and lay still. Furious, Nate scanned the area for a Blood he could shoot only to find there were no other men in sight, Bloods or

Shoshones. He kneed his stallion forward, alert for adversaries, and covered 20 yards without seeing a soul. Then he came to a wide clearing and discovered six Bloods lying sprawled in the positions their bodies had assumed when death claimed them. He halted to get his bearings.

To the northwest arose a few shouts. Otherwise, the battle seemed to have wound down.

Was it truly over? Nate reflected hopefully. Another mounted warrior materialized in the trees across the clearing. It was Spotted Bull, riding proudly, a bloody tomahawk in his right hand, his bow and arrows slung over his back, untouched.

"Hello, Grizzly Killer," the Shoshone said and smiled. "It was a good fight."

Nate said nothing. He would have much rather avoided the bloodshed.

"Touch The Clouds and the others are chasing the few Bloods still alive back toward their own territory," Spotted Bull said. "They will be fortunate if one of them survives to tell of their great defeat."

"Your own people will be quite proud," Nate said politely.

"There will be much rejoicing," Spotted Bull agreed. He stopped next to one of the dead Bloods and dismounted. "This one is mine. How many did you slay?"

Nate had to think before he answered. "Three."

"Truly you are a mighty fighter," Spotted Bull said. "I only killed two myself." He stuck the tomahawk under the leather cord supporting his pants and drew his butcher knife. "You should take their scalps right away, while the flesh is still warm and soft and easy to slice."

"I will," Nate said, and turned the stallion. He'd witnessed enough scalp taking to last him a lifetime and had no desire to watch Spotted Bull take another.

Back into the trees he went, pondering what to do
about the trophies he had earned. If he didn't take the
hair of the men he'd shot, the Shoshones would
wonder about his manhood. Every warrior was expected to take scalps and keep them as mementos of
his prowess in battle. Not to do so was a serious breach
of the unwritten warrior code of conduct to which
every Shoshone male subscribed.

He came to the spot where the third Blood he'd shot
still lay and stared down at the body, torn between his
responsibilities as an adopted Shoshone and his repug-
nance at the thought of scalping a corpse. He'd taken a
few scalps himself in the past, but he still couldn't
accept the practice as necessary or desirable. Of the
few Indian customs that he viewed as truly barbaric,
scalping was the worst.

Voices sounded, and he knew the rest of the Shoshones were on their way back. They would soon be there,
and would no doubt inquire as to why he wasn't taking
the scalps to which he was entitled. They would surely
laugh if they found that the great Grizzly Killer was
afraid to take a little hair.

Nate swung down, stuck the pistol under his belt
again, and carefully placed the rifle on the ground. He
drew his knife, knelt, seized the Blood's long hair in
his free hand, and inserted the tip of the blade under
the skin at the top of the man's forehead. Blood seeped
out, and he had to gird himself before he could make
the first precise incision. He cut methodically, separat-
ing enough of the scalp from the head that the rest
could be lifted in a quick motion once the knife had
completed its grisly handiwork. Gore spattered onto
his leggings and moccasins as the prize dangled in his
grip, and he thought for a second that he might be sick.

One down, two to go.

He went to each of his remaining victims and
appropriated their hair, and as he finished with the last

Blood the Shoshones drifted back. He cut off a strip of fringe from his buckskin shirt and used it to tie the scalps to his saddle horn, where the air would soon have them dry and ready for storage in his saddlebags.

Red Hawk rode up. "This day has made me proud that the Shoshones have accepted me into their tribe," he signed. "They are brave warriors, as brave as any Oglala who ever lived."

"That they are," Nate said.

Red Hawk nodded at the scalps. "You killed three. So did I. This has been a great day for both of us."

"I'll never forget it."

"There is only one thing I regret," Red Hawk said.

"What?"

"That there were not more Bloods. I would have been glad to kill three or four more."

"There will be other days."

The Oglala smiled. "That is what I like about you, Grizzly Killer. You always look at the good side of things."

Chapter Sixteen

The Shoshones lost seven warriors, which was not considered a high price to pay for the hair of 21 Bloods. Spotted Bull held a council to decide what to do with the bodies of their fallen friends. Ordinarily, Shoshone warriors could expect elaborate burials. But when they died on raids or while out hunting far from their village, they were frequently committed to the earth at the first convenient spot. In this case, since the hunting party had traveled less than two sleeps from the village, and since the entire village was on the march and had narrowed the distance even farther, it was unanimously decided to have six warriors take the bodies back. This left 28, including Nate, to go on in search of the buffalo.

Spotted Bull pointed out that it meant their fellow tribesmen would stop for a day to properly dispatch the fallen to the spirit realm. So it would be at least one sleep longer before the members of the hunting party saw their loved ones again. The delay, he stressed, couldn't be helped. None of the warriors complained.

Nate would have liked to be one of those taking the bodies back so he could see Winona and Zachary. But he wasn't asked and didn't think it proper to volunteer his services when he had specifically been invited along as a guest of honor. He helped drape the deceased over their war-horses, then stood enviously watching the six warriors lead the animals off.

The band mounted up and resumed their trek eastward. Hours later, almost at nightfall, they came to a pond and Spotted Bull called a halt. Several warriors went off after game while the rest started fires and tended the horses.

Nate assisted Red Hawk in watering a number of animals, and as he worked, he reflected. On the long ride to the pond he had listened to the warriors proudly relating their exploits during the battle, and he found himself speculating on why he couldn't enter into the spirit of things, why slaying enemies sometimes bothered him so much. He'd lost track of the number of men he'd killed since taking up residence in the Rockies. Some, such as the many Blackfeet he'd slain, didn't upset him in the least. Others, like the Bloods, did. But he couldn't figure out why.

"Is something wrong, Grizzly Killer?" Red Hawk signed.

Nate realized the warrior was studying him intently. He was about to lie, to sign everything was fine, when he changed his mind. "Does killing men ever bother you?" he asked.

The Oglala's eyes narrowed. "Yes," he answered without hesitation.

"It does?"

"A warrior would have to possess a heart of stone not to be affected by the taking of another life. When I was a child, I was taught to have deep reverence for all living things, and especially for those things I kill. If I shoot a deer, I always give thanks to the Everywhere Spirit for the gift of the life I had taken."

"But a man isn't a deer."

"True. I killed my first man, a member of a Cheyenne raiding party who was trying to steal some of our horses, when I was only twelve winters old. For the longest time the deed upset me, and I would have terrible dreams of the man lying in the dust with my arrow in his eye socket and raising his arm to point an accusing finger at me. Finally, when I was older, I went off on a vision quest, and the vision I saw cured me of the terrible dreams forever."

Nate knew of such quests, of how young Indian men and women would go off by themselves to remote spots and fast or commit self-torture in the hope of being visited by a supernatural being who would become the personal guardian spirit of that youth for the remainder of his or her days. The guardian instructed the seeker in proper behavior and in how to perform rituals that would foster health and happiness. "What happened?" he asked.

Red Hawk gazed into the distance. "I saw many strange and wondrous things, but one of the most amazing was the great fiery vulture."

"A vulture?"

"Yes. I saw a field, and on it lay many dead warriors. Then the vulture appeared, flying out of the sun to swoop down and land in the middle of all those dead men. As I watched, the bird began eating their flesh, wolfing it down in huge gulps. As soon as it was done with one body, it would turn to the next. And so it went, on and on, until the vulture had eaten every last warrior."

"And then?" Nate said when the Oglala stopped.

"The vulture kept looking for more bodies to eat, but there were none. It looked and looked, becoming more and more desperate, running this way and that, until finally it grew weak and collapsed from lack of food," Red Hawk said. "I wondered why it did not just fly back up into the sun, but visions are like that. They are not always logical."

Nate didn't see the significance of the vision, but he refused to offend his friend by saying so.

"I thought about it for a long time, and then the meaning became clear."

"It did?"

"Men are meant to die. All men do, sooner or later. Whether they die in their blankets at an old age or die in battle while young, their destiny is all the same. We are all food for the vultures. If men were to stop dying, it would upset the natural order of things."

"But how did this help you get over being upset when you killed another person?"

"Don't you see? Men have been killing each other since the dawn of time. It is natural for men to kill, as natural as eating or sleeping or loving a woman. Yes, slaying another man bothers me, but only if I forget to keep in mind that when I kill I am doing one of the things I was created to do," Red Hawk signed and stared expectantly at Nate. "Do you understand?"

"Yes," Nate replied, although in all truth he didn't. He refused to accept the tenet that men were natural-born killers, predators no different from the grizzly and the mountain lion. There had to be more to humanity. There had to.

"You still appear troubled," Red Hawk said.

"I am," Nate said. "You see, when I was young, I was taught that a man should never kill. Never. It is one of the ten great laws of my people."

"Really?" Red Hawk asked in surprise. "Why is it, then, that so few white men I know follow it?"

"Because my people love to have laws they can break."

"That makes no sense."

"Few things do in this world," Nate muttered, then signed clearly, "I was taught that when a man kills and violates the great law, he displeases the Everywhere Spirit. He will end up in—" Nate paused, trying to find a comparable sign for the concept of Hell. There was none.

"End up where?"

"In a place where people are made to suffer for all time, where they burn in flames that never go out and their cries of agony are never answered."

"Your people truly believe this?"

"Many do."

"The more I learn about your people, the less I understand them. How can mature men hold such a belief when everyone knows that in the spirit world there is no pain or suffering?"

Nate was tempted to point out that a belief in Hell was no stranger than believing in the spiritual significance of visions that included bizarre apparitions such as the fiery vulture, but he held his tongue. What difference did it make? They could discuss the issue until winter, and it would not alter his confusion over killing. Maybe one day he'd find the answer he sought. Until then, he would simply live his life as best he knew how, kill only when put upon, and pray he didn't jeopardize the status of his eternal soul in the bargain. To conclude their talk, he signed, "There is no explaining the things people will believe in." Then he devoted his attention to watering more horses.

The men who had gone out hunting returned with a black-tailed buck, and in due course the aroma of roasting meat wafted on the sluggish breeze. In good spirits, the Shoshones talked and joked until late.

Nate ate his fill, then idly listened to the conversations while thinking about Winona and their son. After the surround—provided he survived—he would take them back to their cabin, and he planned to stop at

Shakespeare's en route. Maybe he would be able to prevail on his mentor to come for a visit. Winona would enjoy having Shakespeare's wife for company, and he could avail himself of the grizzled mountaineer's wisdom. He spent the hours until midnight reviewing the varied and hair-raising adventures that had befallen him since journeying west of the Mississippi River. At last, he wrapped up his introspection by marveling that he had lived as long as he had.

The odds were against him in the long run.

It was common knowledge that few of the white men who entered the uncharted wilderness to take up the trapping trade lasted very long at their new profession. Most perished within two years. Those who lasted three or more were considered old-timers. And rare men like Shakespeare, who had lasted decades, were living legends, widely respected for their store of valuable knowledge as well as their unwavering persistence and iron fortitude.

Nate well knew the risks. But he wasn't about to give up a way of life that totally satisfied every craving of his inner nature. Since coming to the mountains he had found true freedom, genuine peace of mind, and more adventure than most men underwent in their entire lifetimes. Despite the chronic dangers, he felt at home in the Rockies. The wilderness wasn't so much a harsh taskmaster as an instructive tutor. If he kept his wits about him and avoided becoming food for a wandering grizzly or losing his hair to hostiles, he stood one day to be as Shakespeare now was—the epitome of the natural man, rugged and independent and, above all, wise.

There were worse fates.

The next morning the chirping of sparrows brought Nate out of heavy sleep half an hour before sunrise. He sat up, stretched, and noticed he was the first one up except for the sentry. The fire was still going strong. He rose, grabbed the Hawken, and walked into the brush to relieve himself.

All around him the wild creatures were stirring, brought to life by the faint rays of light rimming the eastern horizon. Birds broke into song. The insects buzzed.

Once done, he strolled back to the camp and took a handful of jerky from his saddlebags, then knelt by the fire and ate, enjoying the pungent odor of the burning wood and the warmth on his exposed skin. A few of the Shoshones were snoring. He surveyed the camp, seeing the dozens of buckskin-clad figures with their bows and lances close at hand in case of an emergency. For a fleeting interval he lost all sense of time and place. He had the illusion of being cast back into a primitive era before the coming of the white man to the shores of North America, of being stripped of every last vestige of civilization, of being primitive and in harmony with Nature. He felt as if he was as much a part of the wild as the trees and the beasts. Then Touch The Clouds snorted and sat up and the moment was ruined.

"Grizzly Killer! You are awake early."

"Good morning," Nate said.

The giant yawned and gazed at the gradually brightening sky. "By tonight we should be close to the big buffalo herds. I can hardly wait."

"I am looking forward to finding them also," Nate said to hold up his end of the conversation, and he abruptly realized he really *was* anticipating the upcoming hunt with keen relish. He didn't know of any other white man, not even Shakespeare, who had been on a surround. That thought brought a tingle to his spine. Think of it, he told himself. The first white man ever to do such a thing. The more he thought about it, the more excited he became.

It was not long before all of the Shoshones were up

and prepared to depart. Again Spotted Bull took the lead, and Nate fell in on the warrior's right. During the morning hours little was said. At midday they halted briefly at a stream, then went on. Spotted Bull began relating tales from his youth, and for hours Nate listened in fascination to accounts of how it was in the Rockies long before the arrival of the white man. The Indians had lived much as they did now, as they had for more years than anyone could count. They roamed where they pleased, accountable to no one. Tribe had fought tribe. Warriors had married maidens and reared children. The cycle of life went on as it ever had. For the first time in his life, Nate viewed his own existence as a tiny drop in the river of history. He seemed so small and insignificant when compared to the unfolding tapestry of infinity.   .

The terrain changed as the day progressed. There were fewer high mountains and more hills. By the afternoon they were in the midst of the foothills bordering the Rockies, and occasionally they glimpsed the plains beyond.

Suppressed excitement animated the Shoshones the closer they drew to their destination. When, a few hours before dark, the scouts raced back to announce that the grasslands were right up ahead, the band broke into whoops of delight and urged their mounts into a mass gallop.

Nate whooped with the loudest of them and waved his Hawken overhead. Although he had once crossed the plains to reach the Rockies, he had forgotten how vast the flatlands were, but was vividly reminded when the hunting party emerged from between two hills and halted at the edge of a sea of waving grass that stretched eastward as far as the eye could see.

"We have arrived," Spotted Bull said and nodded in satisfaction. "Tomorrow the hunt begins."

Chapter Seventeen

Nate could barely sleep. Many of the warriors were the same way, tossing and turning in their blankets and muttering to themselves at their inability to rein in their surging emotions. He was lying on his back, his head propped on his hands, when dawn broke, and he leaped to his feet as soon as the first warrior did.

Few were interested in breakfast. Spotted Bull divided the band into four groups with instructions to fan out in different directions in search of a large herd.

Nate found himself in a group with Touch The Clouds, Red Hawk, Drags The Rope, Worm, Lone Wolf, and a warrior named Eagle Claw. He suspected that Spotted Bull deliberately placed him with men he knew well, out of kindness, no doubt, and was grateful for the consideration.

Touch The Clouds led them northward along the fringe of the forest. After an hour a few dark dots appeared to the northeast, and the giant promptly halted.

"Buffalo," he said.

"Do we try and get closer?" Nate asked.

"Not yet," Touch The Clouds said. "We do not want to spook them. They would run back to their herd and might in turn spook the whole bunch." He paused. "Have you ever seen buffalo stampede?"

"No."

"They do not stop for anything until they have totally worn themselves out. We would end up chasing them for a day and a night. I would rather keep the herd close to the foothills to make it easier on our women when the time comes to butcher those we slay."

"I understand."

"We will swing around them and seek the rest," Touch The Clouds said and started off.

Nate anxiously scanned the prairie for more dots. He counted five to the northeast; that was all. There were low hills a few miles past the quintet, and he wondered if the main body might be concealed on the opposite side.

Touch The Clouds angled away from the forest, making a loop to the north of the five beasts, and headed toward those hills.

A warm breeze fanned Nate's face as he rode, stirring his long hair, reminding him of the scalps he had tied to his saddle horn the day before. They were still there, swaying with the rolling gait of the stallion. He touched them, running his fingers through the soft strands and feeling the consistency of the skin at the base of each trophy. They were dry. Later he would stuff them into his saddlebags, and when he got back to the cabin, he would add them to the string of those he had previously taken.

When Touch The Clouds neared the first hill, he slowed and raised an arm to indicate caution. Hunching low over his mount, he advanced.

Nate imitated the giant's example. He held the rifle

low at his side to prevent the sun from glinting off the metal and advertising his presence. Although he hoped to find more buffalo over the crest, he knew that strays often wandered miles from any given herd and that he shouldn't be surprised to find the plain beyond empty.

It wasn't.

Nate came to the top a few steps behind the giant, then halted in dumfounded astonishment at the spectacle of a veritable shaggy carpet of grunting, sniffing brutes that extended for countless miles into the distance. There were thousands and thousands of buffalo—perhaps hundreds of thousands. He heard someone gasp, then realized he had been the one.

Once before Nate had seen a herd, when on his way from St. Louis to the Rockies with his Uncle Zeke. That herd had seemed immense at the time, but it paled into inconsequential puniness when compared with the herd now spread out before his wide eyes. It gave him the willies to see so many enormous beasts congregated together, and he shuddered to think what would happen should they suddenly stampede in his direction. Winona would never find all the tiny pieces.

The males were magnificent, standing over six feet high at the shoulders and weighing about 2000 pounds. The females were only slightly smaller. Both possessed scruffy beards, shaggy manes, and a dark-brown hue. Wicked black horns forked out from their huge heads, with a spread of a yard from horn tip to horn tip. Large humps on their backs, above the shoulders, contained fat that Indians rated a delicacy. The tongue of a buffalo was given the same distinction.

Nate tried to recall everything his uncle had told him about the brutes. They had poor eyesight, but compensated with a sharp sense of smell. They were fierce when provoked and could rip a man or a horse wide open with a single swipe of their horns. Not very intelligent, they would let themselves be driven off of cliffs or run in circles, which would make it possible for the Indians to use the surround as a hunting tactic.

Nate also recollected being told that their skulls were almost impervious to a ball or an arrow. The bone covering the brain was massive and thick. To slay one of the beasts, a hunter must go for the lungs or the heart. "Aim just behind the last rib," Uncle Zeke had advised.

Easier said than done.

Once a buffalo was in motion, racing along as rapidly as a horse, trying to get a bead on the proper spot to hit was a damned difficult task. And even if a hit was scored, there was no guarantee the buffalo would go down. It might keep going for miles, or it might turn on its attacker and charge. As Nate well knew, there were few sights as fearsome as that of having a 2000-pound enraged behemoth barreling straight at you.

He saw several bulls glance up at the top of the hill and tensed. But they simply stared for a bit, then resumed grazing, their large teeth chomping the grass to bits. There were a few calves among the adults, distinguished by their reddish coats. In another month there would be many more. May was the month when most of the females delivered their young.

Touch The Clouds turned his horse, motioned for them to follow, and went to the bottom of the hill. Once there he straightened and beamed. "My father will be very pleased. We have found the main herd. Now two of us must stay here and keep watch while the rest of us go tell my father and the others."

"I'll stay," Nate said impulsively.

Red Hawk lifted his hands to address them in sign. "I wish I spoke your tongue so I could know what is happening."

Nate translated, and the Oglala promptly offered to stay with him.

"Very well," Touch The Clouds said. "Keep out of

sight. If the herd moves, trail them. We will set up a camp at the point where we first came out of the forest. By evening I will send two men to relieve you." He scanned the prairie on all sides. "And stay alert for warriors from other tribes."

"You can count on that," Nate said, then watched the giant lead the rest to the southwest. Drags The Rope waved and Nate waved back. In minutes he was alone with Red Hawk, just two more dots in the limitless expanse of grassland.

"We can take turns lying at the top of the hill," the Oglala signed. "That way if the herd begins to move, we will know right away."

"I will take the first turn," Nate said and slid down from his horse. He handed the reins to his friend and padded up the slope until his head was just below the rim. Flattening, he crawled forward until he could view the herd in all its primeval glory. He made himself comfortable, placing the Hawken at his side and resting his chin on his forearms.

The buffalo were engaged in the varied activities of their species; standing idly, feeding on the lush grass, swatting flies from their thick flanks with swipes of their long, thin tails, or rolling in wallows. The bulls created the latter by gouging their horns in the earth until they had turned over a large circle of sod. Once the soil was exposed to their satisfaction, they would urinate on the dirt, turning the exposed area into mud. Then they would lie down and roll over and over, caking their coats with a muddy layer that temporarily kept insect pests from bothering them.

Nate's initial excitement subsided. As he observed the buffalo over the next few hours, he came to realize his uncle had been absolutely right. They were dumb brutes, nothing more. The mystique they had held for him evaporated in the light of knowledge that they were little different from ordinary cattle. Although they were bigger and stronger and inherently wild, their temperament and behavior were much like their domesticated bovine cousins.

Only once in the time he spent on the hill did anything of significance occur. There was a commotion among the buffalo to his north, and he looked to see a pack of eight white wolves warily approaching the herd.

Immediately, a line of bulls formed at the perimeter while the cows and calves moved deeper into the multitude. The bulls planted their hooves, lowered their heads, and bellowed their warnings to the intruders.

Nate had heard tell that buffalo did not fear any predators except man. He now saw this demonstrated as the wolves halted and contemplated the wall of sinew and the dozens of horns confronting them. One of the wolves yipped, and the entire pack swung to the northwest and loped off toward the foothills. The bulls soon went about their business as if nothing had happened.

Later, as Nate began to doze, he heard light footsteps behind him and looked over his shoulder.

Red Hawk was creeping to the rim. "It is my turn," he signed.

"Have fun," Nate said and went down the hill to the horses. The Oglala had ground-hitched them and they were standing still in the warm sunlight, swatting their tails or flicking an ear every now and then to ward off bugs. He reclined on his back nearby, put his head in his hands, and passed the time thinking about Winona and Zachary.

It was odd, he reflected, that every time he thought about his son he did so using the boy's English name. But Zachary was part Shoshone, and the Indians would always call him Stalking Coyote. It made sense, therefore, for Winona and him to use the boy's Indian name most of the time. He would have to constantly remind himself of that. Old habits were difficult to break.

The afternoon dragged on. Nate dozed some more. Several times he sat up and scoured the prairie for sign of hostiles, but all he saw were a few wolves in the distance and hawks high in the sky. He was relieved when he finally heard horses approaching from the southwest and stood up to discover Drags The Rope and Worm returning.

"Greetings again, Grizzly Killer," Drags The Rope said when they stopped. He grinned. "Did you scare the buffalo off?"

"I tried," Nate said. "Fired my rifle a few times and shouted my head off, but they just looked at me as if I was crazy."

The Shoshones laughed and dismounted.

"Spotted Bull has set up camp," Drags The Rope said and indicated their back trail with a bob of his head. "Ride just a little ways and you will see the smoke from their fire."

Nate rotated, intending to fetch Red Hawk, but the Oglala was already walking toward them. He stepped to the stallion and took hold of its reins. "Try to stay awake," Nate said. "Watching over buffalo has got to be the most boring job a man can have."

"Once our people get here, it will become more exciting than you can imagine," Drags The Rope said.

Nate swung onto his horse. That was the problem, he mused. He could imagine what would happen, and the prospect chilled him to the marrow. But—and the good Lord preserve him—it also thrilled him, and he anticipated the surround with intense expectation. Was he a fool? Or was he merely becoming more like his Indian friends every day?

He waited until Red Hawk mounted, then headed for the camp, looking forward to a hot meal. After traveling 100 yards, the Oglala nudged his arm to get his attention.

"Grizzly Killer, there is something I would like to tell you," Red Hawk signed solemnly.

Nate waited.

"It is about the reason I was cast out of my tribe."

Surprised, Nate responded, "There is no need. Your personal affairs are your own."

"There is a need," Red Hawk said. "I would like you to know, just in case."

"In case what?"

The warrior ignored the question. "I told you that I killed an unarmed man. I did not explain why." He paused, his features shifting, registering profound inner torment. "I was married to a lovely woman, the prettiest in our tribe. Her name is Raven Woman. She and I planned to have many children. I wanted nothing more than to please her and prosper."

Nate said nothing when the Oglala stopped. He had a feeling he knew why Red Hawk was unburdening himself, and he didn't like it at all.

"Our life together was happy until another warrior, High Backed Bear, took an interest in her. He was wealthy. He owned hundreds of horses and already had two wives. But he was not satisfied with what he had."

The ending of the story became obvious. Nate bowed his head in sympathy.

"He took to visiting my wife while I was away. I had no idea until a friend confided in me. When I confronted her, she told me that she loved High Backed Bear and wanted to live in his lodge," Red Hawk said, his hands moving slowly. "Under our law, I should have let her go. I could have thrown her away publicly, and she would then have been free to go to High Backed Bear. No one would have blamed me." He stopped and sighed. "But I was a fool. I would not let her go. So she told me she was going to leave me and go live with her parents."

Nate nodded knowingly. An Indian woman could divorce her husband simply by packing up her things and moving back in with her father and mother. Had Raven Woman done so, Red Hawk would have had no grounds for interfering in her desire to live with High Backed Bear.

"She piled her belongings outside our lodge. Her father and brother came to help carry them. So did High Backed Bear," Red Hawk signed. "I should have ignored him and let them go their way in peace. But he looked at me as she was walking off, looked at me and laughed, and something inside of me snapped. Before I knew what I was doing, I had my tomahawk in my hand and attacked. He tried to back away, but I was too fast."

The Oglala let his hands slump, his story concluded.

"Thank you for telling me," Nate signed. "If it is any consolation, I might have done the same thing if it had happened to me."

"I pray it never does. When a wife does such a terrible thing, it twists a man's insides apart. My heart would not stop weeping."

"You should try to put the past behind you," Nate said in an attempt to cheer his friend up. "You have a second chance on life now. Willow Woman would make a fine wife."

"I know," Red Hawk signed, the corners of his mouth twitching upward. "I plan to ask her after the surround. All I have to do is survive."

That makes two of us, Nate thought.

That makes two of us.

Chapter Eighteen

It took six days for the rest of the Shoshones to arrive at the edge of the foothills. All that time, working in rotation, Spotted Bull's band kept watch over the enormous herd. Two men at a time, day and night, rain or shine, hot or cold, were always close to the buffalo. The herd drifted slowly eastward, and at the end of the six days had gone a distance of 14 miles. With the green grass in abundant supply, the mighty brutes were in no hurry to go elsewhere.

Nate alternated between bothersome boredom when on watch at the herd and avid interest in getting to know the Shoshones better during those hours spent at camp or while out hunting. He spent a lot of time, in particular, in the company of Drags The Rope and Worm. The three of them took it upon themselves to teach Red Hawk the Shoshone language, and Nate was amazed at how readily the Oglala learned it.

Despite the boredom, the time passed quickly. He

was elated when on the afternoon of the seventh day several warriors arrived at the camp to inform Spotted Bull that the lodges were set up not far to the west. A rider was sent to tell the two men on herd duty, and then all the warriors hastened to the encampment.

Nate rode at the head of the band beside Spotted Bull, scarcely able to contain his excitement. The wives of the members of the hunting party were gathered on the east side of the village to greet their husbands, and he spotted Winona the moment the band emerged from the trees. She spied him and dashed forward, Stalking Coyote cradled in her arms, snug in a blanket.

Oblivious to everyone else, Nate reined up, jumped to the ground, and ran to meet her. "I missed you," he said and embraced her, being careful not to squeeze the baby between them. For the longest while they merely stood there, their cheeks touching, their breath soft.

"I missed you too," Winona said. "When I heard about the Bloods, I was afraid for your life."

"Didn't the men who brought the bodies back let you know I was alive?"

"Yes. I still worried."

"I'm here now. There's nothing to worry about."

"Yes, there is."

Nate didn't bother to ask her what that might be. He knew. "How is our son?" he asked to change the subject.

"Take a look," Winona said, stepping back and parting the blanket so he could see their son's face. Stalking Coyote was awake and staring at the world in innocent wonder.

"My son," Nate said and kissed the boy on the forehead. A shadow suddenly fell over them, and he glanced up. Touch The Clouds was a few feet away, astride his huge mount.

The giant beamed. "Tomorrow is the big day, Grizzly Killer," he said, hefting his lance. "My father wants everyone ready to leave at first light."

"I will be set to go," Nate said and felt Winona's fingers dig into his arm. Touch The Clouds moved off, and Nate gazed into his wife's eyes.

Neither said a word.

Dawn bathed the eastern half of the sky in a rosy glow. The Shoshone camp was astir before first light, with the warriors who were going on the surround tending to their horses and triple-checking their weapons while the women of the village sharpened their knives and prepared for the work they would do once the men were done.

Winona gave Nate a kiss that might have lingered until noon had he not gently pushed away and climbed on his horse. He nodded once, then rode off without a backward glance.

Spotted Bull and 34 warriors were waiting near the forest. No one spoke as Nate joined them, and in a body they swung eastward, making for the prairie, each man a study in somber contemplation.

Nate scarcely noticed the birds in the trees or the cool morning breeze. His mind seemed to be detached from his body, as if it floated above his head and observed the proceedings with detachment. This can't really be happening, he told himself, and yet it was. He would soon be risking life and limb, not to mention his future with the most beautiful woman in the world. Any sane person would bow out, but he rode on.

Spotted Bull picked up the pace when they reached the prairie, and the 14 miles to the herd were covered in grim silence. The two men on watch were concealed in a thin stand of trees a quarter mile from the unsuspecting beasts. Spotted Bull rode into the stand and did not bother to climb down. He moved to the east edge of the stand where he could study the position of the buffalo.

Nate did the same. He noticed a small section of the herd, comprising 300 or 400 animals, was grazing a few hundred yards north of the main body, separated from the rest by a series of low knolls.

Spotted Bull pointed at the small group. "They are the ones we will kill," he said. "Half of you will go with me. The rest will go with my son." He paused and swept over them with a meaningful gaze. "All of you know what to do."

"Except me," Nate said.

"We are going to approach the buffalo from two sides and drive them ahead of us," Spotted Bull said. "Once they are running at full speed, we will try to turn the leaders in upon the rest. If it works, we will slay many." He mustered a smile. "Stick close to me, my friend. You will do fine."

In another minute the band was divided and Touch The Clouds led his men from the stand, heading to the north to get on the far side of the herd. Once there they stopped and the giant waved his lance overhead. Spotted Bull then led Nate and the rest toward the knolls.

Nate figured out the strategy right away. If Spotted Bull could gain the knolls before the buffalo to the north knew what was happening, then the small section would be effectively cut off from the main body and caught between Spotted Bull's men and his son's. Simple, but perfect. Nate tightened his grip on the Hawken and stayed near Spotted Bull at the head of their group, trying to keep his surging emotions in check. His pulse was racing faster than the stallion.

Many of the buffalo on both sides looked up as the Shoshones approached, the bulls adopting their characteristic defiant stance, but they made no attempt to flee. Confident in their might and their numbers for the moment, they held their ground.

Spotted Bull was virtually flying across the plain, and Nate was hard pressed to stay even with the aged warrior. He flowed with the rhythm of the stallion, bent at the waist with his head almost touching the horse's rippling neck. The pounding of many hooves behind him sounded like the distant rumble of thunder.

Nate glanced off to the left, to the north, and saw Touch The Clouds and his men in motion, paralleling Spotted Bull. Both bands were rapidly narrowing the gap, and he wondered how much longer the small section of buffalo would stand firm. The answer came seconds later, at the selfsame instant his group attained the knolls.

Erupting into motion, the buffalo wheeled and fled, and since there were now Shoshones between them and the main herd to the south and more Shoshones to the north, they had no choice but to sprint generally eastward, a few of the biggest bulls taking the lead. Dust swirled skyward from under their driving hooves.

Spotted Bull began whooping wildly and all the Shoshones with him took up the chorus.

Nate did likewise. Gazing out over the rushing beasts, he noticed that Touch The Clouds and the warriors with him were not making any noise. Why not? he wondered, and then the reason occurred to him. Spotted Bull was trying to drive the small section away from the main herd. If Touch The Clouds and those with him were to start making as much noise as the men with Spotted Bull, the buffalo might turn to the south in a frantic effort to regain the safety of the larger body.

As it was, the ploy worked. The hundreds of buffalo in the small section angled to the northeast, at least a third of the small herd well ahead of the pursuing Shoshones on both sides.

A minute elapsed, the race continuing. Nate inhaled dust and tasted it in his mouth. To his consternation, Spotted Bull unexpectedly went faster. He followed suit, riding as he had never before ridden, keenly aware of the warriors to his rear and the stream of buffalo off to his left, not more than 15 yards away and drawing closer bit by bit as Spotted Bull slanted slowly toward them.

Nate risked a quick glance to his right to see if the main herd had moved and saw the whole great multitude in flight to the south. He couldn't afford to watch the spectacle; he had more pressing concerns. Clearly, Spotted Bull was trying to overtake the lead bulls in order to start driving them back into the small herd, and it would take every ounce of stamina and speed their horses possessed to accomplish the feat, not to mention superb skill on the part of the riders.

The 300 or more buffalo were still running hard, exhibiting the sterling endurance for which they were widely noted. Even the calves showed no sign of flagging. The bulls, ever more belligerent and naturally protective, were to the outside of the stampeding horde.

Nate screeched until his throat was raw, then screeched some more. He was pleased to see they were gaining on the herd leaders, but he dreaded what would occur once they caught up with the beasts. Turning such a swarm of massive brutes would be extremely dangerous. Now, more than ever, he understood why so many warriors lost their lives on a surround and why the women of the tribe became anxious at the mere mention of one.

He studied the buffalo, observing their peculiar gait, their bobbing heads, and their relatively short legs driving their enormous bodies, and he found himself wishing there were fewer of the brutes and more Shoshones participating in the chase.

After several more minutes, Nate was almost to the head of the herd. The din was deafening, a cacophony of pounding hooves, snorting brutes, and bleating, frightened calves. He repeatedly glanced at Spotted Bull, waiting for the warrior to cut in toward the lead bulls, knowing if he missed his cue he would overshoot the herd and make a prized fool of himself in the bargain.

Fortunately, Spotted Bull let everyone know his intent by bellowing at the top of his lungs, *"Now!"* Then, jerking on his mount's reins, the Indian galloped at the foremost bulls, yelling and waving like a madman.

Nate immediately performed the same maneuver, his stallion responding superbly, his breath catching in his throat as he galloped straight at the front row of buffalo. Panic seized him, and he thought for a moment that the beasts wouldn't turn, that they would plow into Spotted Bull and himself and probably the rest of the warriors, trampling every last man underfoot in the blink of an eye, reducing the hunters to so much pulp and crushed bone. He could see the lead bulls clearly, see their flared nostrils and their wide, dark eyes, see their sides heaving as they breathed, and see the curved horns that would rend him to pieces should anything go wrong.

Thankfully, no sooner did the hunting party turn than the foremost buffalo tried to flee to the north only to find their way blocked by Touch The Clouds and his men, who were cutting in from their side. Confused, trapped between the two groups of charging warriors, the lead bulls then did as the Shoshones were hoping: they abruptly turned back into the herd. Those following the leaders also turned inward, and the herd swirled in upon itself, in a state of utter confusion, many animals colliding, while a rising cloud of dust added immensely to the bedlam.

Nate saw Spotted Bull take aim with a bow and send a shaft into a bull. The brute staggered but stayed on its feet. A second arrow brought it down; it rolled forward and crashed into a cow. He glanced both ways and suddenly realized he was in the midst of the milling herd, surrounded by 2000-pound monsters, hemmed in with no way out.

Other warriors were in the same situation, and they were loosing arrows or employing lances to deadly effect, striving to slay as many buffalo as they could.

Nate glimpsed more Shoshones riding around the perimeter, trying to contain the disoriented beasts. Then he could not afford the luxury of simply observing; to stay alive he must kill and kill again. He whipped the Hawken to his right shoulder and took a bead on a huge bull nearby. At the sharp report, the bull crumpled onto its forelegs. Eager to finish it off, Nate reined up and started reloading. His fingers closed on the powder horn, and as he went to pour the proper amount of black powder into the palm of his left hand he happened to look to his right and saw another bull bearing down on his stallion with its head lowered, ready to gore and rip.

Chapter Nineteen

Nate hauled on the reins, turning the stallion to one side, and the bull went shooting past, its horn missing the horse by a hair. Expecting the bull to whirl and attack again, he rode behind a petrified cow to buy time to reload. To his amazement, the bull kept on going, ramming another bull instead, and the two took to fighting one another.

His fingers trembling, Nate poured out the powder. He wished he'd thought to ask for a lance. During the seconds he would be preoccupied with loading, he was a sitting target for any beast who spied him.

Be calm! he chided himself. Keep your hands steady! If he lost his nerve now, he was as good as dead. He didn't dare freeze up momentarily, as he'd done with the mountain lion. He must keep firing and riding and pray for the best.

Pandemonium reigned. The buffalo were caught in a muddled maze of their own devising, with animals dashing every which way and having nowhere to go because they were blocked by others of their kind or the Shoshones, who were whooping and killing in reckless abandon, in the grip of a primitive blood lust.

Nate got the Hawken reloaded and looked around for the bull he'd wounded. The animal was nowhere in sight, hidden by the ever thickening shroud of dust. Suddenly a buffalo bumped into his stallion's flank, and he goaded the horse forward but could only go a few feet so dense was the press of baffled brutes. Many buffalo were utterly confounded and stood there in helpless bewilderment, making no move to attack the Shoshones. Other animals, however, seemed to know instinctively just who to blame for their predicament and were charging the warriors as opportunities presented themselves.

Aiming hastily, Nate shot a cow. Reloading hurriedly, he shot another. His hands were a blur as he used the powder horn, reached into the ammunition pouch, and employed the ramrod. Move! Move! Move! he mentally shrieked. To slow down was to die.

He saw the bull he'd wounded and shot it, then moved a yard to reload yet again. The dust temporarily parted and he spotted Worm a dozen yards off, wedged in by buffalo and jabbing to the right and left with a lance. To his horror, an enormous bull lunged at Worm's horse, the curved horns slicing into the poor mount's stomach as easily as a sharp knife through butter. The war-horse threw back its head and neighed in terror, and then the buffalo slammed into it again and the horse went down.

Nate saw Worm leap clear, but now the Shoshone was afoot among the beasts, and Nate frantically kicked his stallion in an attempt to forge through the buffalo and reach the warrior. Worm speared a cow and she keeled over. The Shoshone rotated, his lance upraised for another cast.

Out of the pack came another bull, massive head down, hooves drumming forcefully.

"Worm!" Nate shouted in warning and gripped one of his pistols. The flintlocks wouldn't down a buffalo, but they might distract it. He started to yank the gun free.

Worm turned, saw the charging bull, and went to cast his lance. The bull reached him first, its broad forehead smacking into his chest and lifting him clean off the ground.

Nate distinctly heard the loud crack of Worm's ribs caving in. Blood spurted from the warrior's mouth, and then Worm fell in front of the bull and was lost to sight. Other beasts trampled him.

Appalled, Nate reloaded the Hawken, aimed at a nearby bull, and fired. He didn't know how long he could sustain such a hectic pace. His heart pounded in his chest and there was a roaring in his ears. Ignore it, he admonished himself. He had to ignore everything but the buffalo and shoot them until the rifle barrel became too hot to touch, and maybe he'd survive.

He downed another brute, then another, and lost track of the number he killed from there. Desperately, mechanically, he reloaded and fired, reloaded and fired, reloaded and fired. A small cloud of gunsmoke hovered above him, mixing with the dust. He shot and shot and shot until his hands were sore from shoving the ramrod home and his fingers were caked with grainy gunpowder. And still he shot some more.

Suddenly he noticed the buffalo had thinned out and he had extra space in which to turn the stallion. Either he had emerged from the center of the herd or the animals on the outer edge had fled, allowing those hemmed in the middle to flee. The dust was now so thick he could barely see ten feet in any direction. He spotted a dead horse to his right, but there was no sign of the rider. There were dead buffalo everywhere.

He skirted a convulsing cow and stopped when a Shoshone materialized out of the dust cloud like a ghost out of the fog. It was Spotted Bull, and the warrior smiled.

"Grizzly Killer! My wife will be pleased with her robe!"

Nate grinned, then stiffened when he spied a bull charging at Spotted Bull from the warrior's right side. "Look out!" he cried, goading the stallion forward to try to intercept the beast.

But the buffalo was lightning fast, and it was on Spotted Bull before the man could move his horse out of its path. The brute rammed into the mount, knocking the horse flat. But as the animal went down, Spotted Bull vaulted from its back, landed on his right shoulder, and rolled to his feet, his right hand sweeping an arrow from his quiver.

He never got the shaft off.

Uttering a roar of rage, Touch The Clouds galloped onto the scene, his huge lance held with the sharpened tip down, his muscular body braced for the impact. He never slowed, never deviated from his course, charging the bull as it tried to go after his father. The lance tore into the bull's side just shy of the ribs and sank in over a yard. The bull went berserk, thrashing and tugging to one side, trying to pull loose. Touch The Clouds held on firmly, his features flushed from the herculean exertion. He abruptly changed tactics, urging his horse to step forward, burying the lance farther.

The bull snorted, then went completely rigid and fell on its side with a pronounced thud.

Spotted Bull took two bounds and jumped up onto the back of Touch The Clouds's horse. The giant rode to the left, disappearing in the cloud.

Relieved that his friend was safe, Nate resumed

slaying buffalo, always alert for one that might come after him. He slew four, astounded that so many of the beasts simply stood there while he took their lives. If the Shoshones were having similar luck, he wouldn't be surprised if they decimated the herd.

He rode 15 yards after the fourth kill, seeking to add to his tally, and was surprised to find himself in the clear. There were no buffalo around. Reining up, he looked every which way, trying to see the rest of the herd. To his left the dust had thinned considerably and he saw a lone bull.

The animal wasn't alone.

There were nine wolves ringing the horned behemoth, each snapping and biting at its legs and belly, trying to cripple it and bring it down.

Nate was stunned to see them. He had no idea where they came from. The bull, despite having sustained serious wounds and bleeding profusely in a half-dozen spots, was giving an excellent account of itself. Even as Nate watched, those twin horns of destruction lifted a yowling wolf high into the air, splitting its side. He decided not to interfere in the battle. There were plenty of buffalo to go around, for both humans and wolves.

Turning, he scanned the prairie, or as much of it as was visible in the slowly dispersing dust. He discerned a large animal lying on its side not far off and moved toward it, thinking it might be a buffalo that needed to be put out of its misery. But when he drew close enough, he recognized the animal was a horse.

He stopped next to the mount, frowning at the sight of the nasty gashes in its side, gashes spurting a torrent of blood. A thin crimson trail led from the back of the horse into the dust cloud, leading Nate to surmise a wounded warrior had crawled off to escape the buffalo responsible for the attack.

Nate went around the horse and rode into the cloud,

hoping he could find the man and be of some assistance. Soon he distinguished the prone form of a Shoshone on the ground ahead. He hastened up to the body and, heedless of the danger, dropped to the earth. Kneeling, he gently gripped the warrior's shoulder and rolled the man over.

It wasn't a Shoshone.

Lying as still as a stone, his stomach torn to shreds, his intestines oozing out, was Red Hawk.

"No!" Nate screamed, dropping the Hawken and placing a hand on each side of the Oglala's head. "Not you!"

Red Hawk's eyelids fluttered, then snapped open. He grunted and blinked a few times before focusing on Nate. "Grizzly Killer," he said in Shoshone. "Happy you. Good thing."

"Do not talk," Nate admonished him, unable to stop moisture from filling his eyes. "I will wrap your stomach in my blanket and take you to the village."

Incredibly, Red Hawk grinned weakly. "No. Think not."

"Oh, God," Nate said in English, gaping in horror at the ruptured abdominal cavity. "Oh, sweet God."

"What?" Red Hawk asked, again using Shoshone.

"I do not want you to die," Nate said, choking on his words, swallowing hard when he was done.

"All die, Grizzly Killer," Red Hawk said. He coughed and grimaced.

"There must be something I can do," Nate said forlornly. Ineffable sorrow racked him, and he bit his lower lip to keep from crying.

"Remember me."

"I will," Nate promised. "Always."

Red Hawk coughed louder, and crimson drops formed at both corners of his mouth. "Not long," he breathed. His eyelids fluttered a second time. He wheezed, then regained full consciousness and stared intently at Nate. "One thing do me. Please."

"Anything. Anything at all."

"Tell Willow Woman—" Red Hawk began and stopped to groan and shiver. He took a deep breath and continued swiftly. "Tell Willow Woman I sorry. Love her much."

Nate tried to respond but his throat was strangely constricted.

"Please," Red Hawk said.

"I will," Nate croaked.

A serene expression came over Red Hawk's face and he smiled. "Thank you, friend. Thank you."

Nate felt the Oglala stiffen and saw Red Hawk's eyes go blank. "No!" he wailed and violently shook his friend's head, trying to shake the life back into him, shaking until his arms were so tired they could barely move. He belatedly realized what he was doing and ceased, aghast. A soul-wrenching sob tore from his lips and was carried on the sluggish breeze.

He heard a snort and grabbed the Hawken, his misery curtailed by the realization he might be in great peril. Surging upright, he spun and was astounded to see that the dust cloud had for the most part dispersed. He could see the prairie and the aftermath of the surround, and he could scarcely credit the testimony of his own eyes. It was as if Ares, the ancient Greek god of war had paid the earth a visit and waged battle with a horde of shaggy brutes. The prairie resembled a battlefield. No—it was a battlefield, and the soil in many places now bore a scarlet tinge. Scores of buffalo lay dying or dead, many in pools of blood. Dozens of wounded animals staggered in a vain attempt to run or stood with red rivulets pouring from their wounds. Here and there were fallen horses. And mingled among the animals were the bodies of five Shoshones.

Five Shoshones and one Oglala.

* * *

Three weeks later.

"I am sorry to see you go," Spotted Bull said sincerely. "We have enjoyed your company."

Nate, astride the stallion, hefted the Hawken and looked down at his host. Beside Spotted Bull stood Morning Dove, her fine new robe over her slender shoulders. A few feet to their rear, next to the lodge entrance, was Willow Woman. "We can never thank you enough for your kindness and hospitality," he said. "I hope you will permit us to return the favor one day by paying us a visit at our wooden lodge."

"We will," Spotted Bull promised. "I would like to see your unusual lodge for myself. Perhaps then I will understand why a man would build a lodge that must always stay in the same spot."

"Come whenever you want," Winona said. She sat on the mare, Stalking Coyote in a cradleboard strapped to her back. "Our home is your home."

Nate smiled, wheeled the stallion, and grasped the lead to their pack animal securely in his left hand. He rode southward, winding among the lodges, and didn't speak again until they had left the village a good distance behind. "At last," he said in English, glancing at Winona. "I like your kin and all, but we should have left a week or so ago."

"My aunt insisted that we stay a little longer. How could we refuse?"

"Are you upset that we're leaving now?" Nate asked. "We can turn around and go back, if you want."

Winona shook her head. "No. I am as eager to reach our cabin as you are."

"Are you certain?" Nate pressed her, well aware of her tendency to keep things that upset her to herself so she wouldn't in turn upset him.

"Yes," Winona said. "It is well we left now, before Willow Woman had a chance to talk to you."

"Willow Woman?" Nate said in surprise. "What did she want to talk to me about?"

"She wanted to ask you a question," Winona said, her tone betraying a degree of annoyance. "And I would rather not discuss it."

"Why not?"

"Because I have already decided what your answer to her would be," Winona said, gazing straight ahead.

"That's nice of you," Nate said, grinning. "Then there isn't any harm in telling me, is there?"

Winona looked at him and pursed her lips. "All right. I will let you know, only because you will pester me forever if I do not."

Nate waited.

"She was going to ask you if you would be interested in having two wives," Winona said in a rush.

Thinking that his wife was joking, Nate was about to laugh when he saw the anger in her eyes and knew she was serious. He also understood why she was so glad to be departing. Then, knowing full well he might have to spend a few nights sleeping on the floor when they got home, he asked a question of his own, struggling to stay composed. "What did you decide, anyway?"